FOR OUR CHILDREN'S SAKE

BY

NATASHA OAKLEY

MILLS & BOON®

© Natasha Oakley 2004

ISBN 0 263 18530 3

Set in Times Roman 16¼ on 17½ pt.
16-0205-52381

Printed and bound in Great Britain
by Antony Rowe Ltd, Chippenham, Wiltshire

FOR OUR
CHILDREN'S SAKE

CHAPTER ONE

IT WAS all true. All of it. Until this moment Lucy Grayford hadn't allowed herself to believe it. All the way from Shropshire she'd told herself there'd been some kind of mistake. Some different universe she'd stumbled into and would surely soon stumble out of. But, looking at the deeply troubled man opposite, she knew there'd been no mistake—not this time.

With immense effort she tried to concentrate on what he was trying to tell her. She could see his mouth moving and yet it was so difficult to take the words in. What they really meant. To her. To Chloe.

'Genetically, Chloe isn't your child,' Dr Shorrock said carefully. Very, very carefully, she registered bleakly. Every word predetermined and carefully phrased. 'The embryos implanted back into your womb belonged to another couple.'

It should hurt more.

Surely this kind of news was something you couldn't stay sane through.

'But...but I gave birth to Chloe.' Her mind struggled to come to terms with what he was saying. She *had* given birth to Chloe. Eleven long hours and seventeen stitches later she'd had a seven pound, fourteen ounce little girl. She'd held her in her arms immediately after—red, wrinkled and unbelievably perfect. And hers.

From that moment her life had revolved around the miracle of her baby.

'This is difficult to understand, Mrs Grayford, I know.' The steady voice of Dr Shorrock faltered and his fingers shuffled nervously at his papers. 'Whilst you carried Chloe to term, and gave birth naturally to her, both the egg and sperm belonged to another couple and—'

'She's mine,' Lucy cut in. This was a nightmare. A hateful clawing nightmare. Slowly the full truth of what he was saying was beginning to penetrate her numb brain. He was trying to tell her Chloe didn't belong with her. That she belonged to another couple.

But if they only knew her as an egg and a sperm surely she belonged with her? It had been her body that had carried her. Her body that had given her life. 'She's been my baby for six years. You can't suddenly say you want her back. That—'

'I'm sorry to say the error was more far-reaching than that.'

There was something about his expression that held Lucy silent. She almost didn't let herself breathe. He'd already brought her world crashing down around her. What could be worse than what he'd already said?

'At the time of the...error...you and your late husband had three good embryos stored at the same clinic.'

The pressure on her heart was almost unbearable as she waited for whatever he was going to say next. 'Yes?' she managed, forcing out the single word through dry lips.

'All three were implanted into the womb of another woman and one resulted in the birth of a healthy baby girl.'

'My baby?' Her voice faltered.

'*Genetically* the baby of yourself and your late husband. Yes.'

Lucy put one shaking hand up to her forehead, trying to rub away the pain that had begun to wrap an iron band around her head. It was impossible to take any of this in. This slightly pompous-looking man with his hair combed over the bald patch on his head was talking about *errors* and *embryos*, and yet what he was really talking about was lives. People's lives. Their lives.

'Naturally a full investigation will be undertaken. At this time I can only offer you our most profound apologies.'

She let her hand fall back into her lap. 'I don't understand. How... How could such a thing happen? It isn't possible.'

'Mistakes are extremely rare in embryology, but there's always the risk of human error. All clinics are required to operate scrupulous labelling systems and to double check embryos before implantation. Although the clinic you attended did have all the correct protocols designed to prevent this from happening, as in all areas of medicine, sometimes things do go wrong.'

'Do the other couple know? Have you told them?'

Dr Shorrock looked back down at his notes before returning his steady gaze to hers. 'A blood test on their daughter showed she has a rhesus negative blood type which revealed there must have been an error. Both her birth parents are rhesus positive so it was obvious she couldn't be their biological child.'

'I'm rhesus negative.' Her hands shook in her lap. She folded them tightly into fists and allowed her nails to dig into her palms. It was good to feel something other than the screaming pain ripping through her head. *Please God… Oh, please God… No.*

She knew what pain felt like. Knew exactly what it felt like to want the world to stop turning and everything disappear into blissful darkness. She'd thought she'd never recover from the agony of losing Michael and yet this was unbelievable. It was as though he'd died all over again and had taken with him the one thing—the one person—who'd been able to console her. The person who'd given her a reason to go on living. Breathing in and out until one day she'd suddenly felt alive again. Happy, even. And yet here she was back in a blackness she hadn't even imagined existed.

'This must be a mistake,' she whispered. 'This can't be happening.'

Dr Shorrock lowered his eyes, as though he couldn't bear to see the pain in hers. 'I'm confident from the tests we've undertaken so far that there was a switch of embryos at the im-

plantation stage. Possibly there was some confusion over the names. And yet—' He broke
off and shook his head in apparent disbelief. 'I
can't give you accurate answers about how this
might have happened. Not before we've undertaken a full investigation and I've received the
report. While that's still pending I want you to
know the head of the unit has been suspended
with immediate effect and all the appropriate
authorities have been informed.'

As if she cared. The people at the clinic were
people she didn't know, didn't care about. But
still he went on, his face a picture of professional concern.

'Obviously there'll be many questions that
need answers and I will be assiduous in asking
them. The—'

'What happens now? To Chloe and me?'

His cheeks puffed out. 'Naturally we must
have the well-being of the girls at the very centre of everything we do. There's no definitive
ruling on how a direct switch of embryos
should be dealt with, although all rulings *do*
suggest you will continue to have guardianship
of Chloe during her minority.'

Guardianship? What did that mean? Chloe was her daughter. Had been from her first breath.

'While the legalities are being debated in court you, yourself, will need to consider what you want to happen. Do you want access to your biological child or not? Ultimately there will have to be a legal ruling on who these children actually belong to.'

His words continued but Lucy was no longer interested. In her heart the words were pounding over and over again. *Chloe's not my daughter. Not my daughter.* And yet she was. In every way that mattered Chloe was her daughter. She'd been the little warm figure who'd cuddled up in that lonely double bed during thunderstorms. She'd been the toddler she'd stayed up all night with when she'd had chicken pox. She was hers. Absolutely. And she would fight for her. With the very last breath she had in her body.

And her other baby? Hers and Michael's. The baby who'd grown up being cuddled and cared for by other people—strangers. Slowly she felt the pressure on her heart increase in a tight, painful grip.

There were no easy answers to this. She felt the trickle of warm tears as they began to fall down her face. She was *crying*. She didn't mean to be crying but the tears came without any help from her. One after another, pouring down her face—and yet soundless.

Dr Shorrock pushed a box of tissues across his desk. 'I do realise how difficult this is for you, Mrs Grayford. For the time being I think you should give yourself a chance to assimilate everything I've told you. Meanwhile I will set in motion some of the things we've agreed upon.'

Agreed? Had they agreed on anything? Lucy really didn't know. She pulled out a tissue and wiped the tears from her face. Pointless, really, as others soon replaced them.

He stopped to write something down in a large manila folder. 'A nurse will give you a cup of tea and sit with you a while. I can only offer my sincere apologies on behalf of my colleagues and tell you I shall be in contact very shortly.'

Dominic Grayling sat on the graffiti-covered wooden bench outside the hospital, his gaze following the movement of people in and out without any real focus. He shouldn't have come, and yet the temptation to be here had been irresistible. He'd told himself a million times since last Friday that the date and time he'd seen marked down on his file might pertain to anything, to anyone. And yet he hadn't believed that, not deep down in his soul. As soon as he'd read what was written it had become inevitable he'd be here. Waiting.

He glanced down at his watch, and then back again at the doors to the hospital. It was late now. Perhaps he'd missed them. He'd been so sure he'd be able to recognise them when he saw them. They'd look like he had when he'd first understood what had happened. They'd be lost. Hurting.

He didn't mean to talk to them. To make any sign at all. He just wanted to know what they looked like. Whether they were nice, he supposed. If he could imagine his biological child living with them and being happy. That would be enough. Surely that would be enough?

The doors opened with an automatic swish and he heard the soft brogue of an Irish accent asking, 'Are you sure you don't want to wait a while longer? I don't like to see you leave like this.'

'I just want to go home. I need to go home now.'

The other voice was strained, choking. It was a voice that touched him. Spoke to the hurt deep within himself.

He turned almost automatically and saw her. She was beautiful. Even though she'd been crying. Was crying, he noticed. She was still beautiful, with brown hair alive with auburn highlights. Curls softly framing an oval face. Exactly like his Abigail.

Dominic forced himself to look away and muttered a short expletive under his breath. He was beginning to go out of his mind. Seeing similarities where there weren't any. London was full of women with dark hair. He might as well stand in Covent Garden and hold up a banner for all the good this was doing. He was looking for a couple.

And yet *he* was alone.

He turned back to watch the woman. Her olive-tinted colouring was similar to Abby's and there'd been no one else who'd seemed possible. She'd pulled her black coat closely around her body and was desperately searching in her pocket for something. A tissue? And all the while her tears continued to fall.

It was her pain that made him watch her. It simply radiated from every pore. It felt like a mirror being held up to his own emotion. The devastating pain he had no words to describe accurately.

Her hand came out empty and she put her fingers up to her eyes, wiping away the trails of moisture. He couldn't bear it—to see her pain and do nothing. He stood up and walked towards her hesitantly, before handing her a starched white handkerchief from his overcoat pocket.

She saw the flash of white before understanding what he was offering. 'I'm sorry… I… I'll be fine in a minute. I'm sorry. It's just I…'

'Take it. It's just a handkerchief,' he said curtly.

'Thank you.' Her fingers closed about it and she wiped at her eyes. Then, with a little confusion, she offered it back to him.

'Keep it.'

She looked back down at the damp fabric in her hand. 'Oh, yes,' she said, before saying helplessly, 'Thank you.'

'It's nothing. My name is Dominic Grayling.'

She looked at him blindly. His name obviously meant nothing to her. Why should it? He wasn't arrogant enough to assume she'd recognise it from the television documentary he'd made two years previously, and even if she were one half of the couple he'd hoped to see there was no reason she should know his name. The hospital had been scrupulous in keeping that information secret. He tried another tack. 'Is there anything I can do to help you?'

She'd begun to shake her head even before he'd finished speaking. 'Nothing. I'll be fine. Thanks for this, though,' she said with a small brave smile, before turning away to walk down the steps.

It was something in the way she smiled, or turned, perhaps, but he couldn't let her go. Dominic quickly walked down the steps beside her. 'I know I shouldn't be doing this, but I have to ask.'

She turned and looked back up at him, her brown eyes troubled and a little scared.

Dominic took a deep breath. He was going to sound stupid but he couldn't let this chance escape him. Before they knew it they were going to be overtaken by people whose concern was the legalities. There was just a small chance for him to take control—now, before all their lives were blighted more than they already were.

'Have you by any chance just been told your daughter isn't yours?' he asked in a rush, before his courage failed. He saw the way her mouth moved in a soundless exclamation and rushed on. 'My wife and I received IVF treatment seven years ago and I've just discovered the embryo used...' He couldn't bring himself to finish the words. 'I'm sorry, I shouldn't have said anything. I'm not even sure what I'm doing here.'

'Lucy Grayford.'

Dominic turned back and looked at her.

'My name is Lucy Grayford,' she said slowly. 'And, yes. Yes, I have.'

They stood in complete silence, each searching for some kind of truth in the face of the other. Dominic took a shaky breath. 'I'm glad to meet you.' He stepped down the final step. 'My name is Dominic Grayling,' he repeated, certain this time she'd actually heard him.

Her eyes never left his face. She was like a scared fawn. Her dark eyes were frightened and her whole body was tense.

'I think perhaps we ought to talk.'

She nodded.

He wanted to put her at ease, and yet what could he say that would make this any easier to bear? It was as though a door had opened to hell itself. And here they were, two strangers brought together by a human tragedy with no easy way to navigate a path through it.

'There's a park around the corner. Perhaps that would be best. There's a place to get coffee nearby. Perhaps that would be better than—' He broke off again. They were complete strangers. Why should she agree to this? He could be anyone. Some strange crank. 'Or would you rather leave it for another time?' He reached into his pocket to pull out a notepad and pen. 'I could give you my number. We could talk later. When you've had time to think about it.' He started to write.

'No.' He looked up as she spoke. She shook her head firmly. 'I don't want to go home yet.'

That was a feeling he understood. He knew how hard it was to discover the child you loved, believed was your own, was not. And, knowing that, you then had to go home and pretend nothing had changed. That the centre of your world hadn't been ripped out and shredded as though it were some discarded document. He'd walked out of this same hospital and wandered in the rain for over two hours before he'd summoned up enough courage to take himself back to Abby.

'I'd rather talk.'

He nodded. With tacit agreement they turned and walked along the pavement. Despite her words neither spoke but, in the strangest way, the silence was comforting.

Lucy put her hands deep in her coat pockets and let the wind dry the tears on her face. The pain had settled deep within her heart and she felt cold. Frightened. Nothing in her life had ever prepared her for this.

Covertly she looked up at Dominic Grayling. In any other circumstances he might have been an attractive kind of man. Handsome, even. He was tall, loose-limbed and wiry, with an intelligent face and kind eyes. Not particularly like Chloe, though, she thought. She was much fairer; her hair was a shining curtain of ash blonde. Yet maybe there was something indefinably like her in this man. Perhaps in the shape of his face? An expression?

Who knew why she'd agreed to talk to him? Surely she'd have been more sensible to wait until the professionals were involved. They'd be able to work out a way through this night-mare. And yet... Dominic's eyes told her he shared her pain, understood what she was feel-ing. Dr Shorrock, with all his calm, professional detachment, hadn't even touched on the agony she was feeling.

'We can get a coffee here.'

His deep voice broke into her thoughts and she looked up to see him pointing across the road at a narrow shop frontage with a chipped sign above reading Sarah's Teas.

'Fine.'

They crossed the road and Dominic held open the door to allow her to pass before him. The shop was full, a lunchtime crowd of busy, bustling people. Some were sitting round mel-amine tables reading newspapers over limp sandwiches. All infuriatingly normal. Yet here she was with her life in tatters.

'How do you like your coffee?'

'Coffee?' she repeated stupidly, until her mind shifted back into gear. Oh, yes, she was going to have coffee. 'White, one sugar.'

Lucy turned back to look at the room and caught sight of herself in the mirror. Her re-flection looked normal. That surprised her. Was that what everyone else saw? *How strange.*

Surely if the world as you knew it had just ended, something of that should show on your face? Was that why everyone had gone on and on saying how well she'd looked after Michael had died? It had puzzled her at the time.

'Coffee.' Dominic's voice interrupted her as he held out a cardboard cup with a plastic lid on top.

Once again his eyes held complete understanding. They were nice eyes. Steely blue with golden flecks like sunshine. You could trust eyes like that. She took the cup. 'Thank you.'

'The park is round the corner. It's not too far.'

Lucy didn't care. She'd have followed him anywhere at this moment. Just knowing she didn't have to make a decision was enough. Her brain couldn't cope with anything. He wanted to walk in a park—she'd walk in a park.

It wasn't much of a park. It was smaller than the ones near her home, surrounded by high iron railings and hemmed in by densely packed housing. The concrete walls of a nearby high-rise were covered with graffiti. An ugly place, she thought with a curious detachment.

'We could sit on the bench over there,' he said, and pointed at a wooden seat underneath some old oak trees. His kind eyes glanced down at her. 'I shouldn't be doing this to you. It's too soon. You're still in shock.'

'I'll always be in shock.'

An almost imperceptible nod of the head before he turned and walked towards the seat.

'Do you want to tell me what they told you?' he asked as she sat next to him.

Lucy shook her head. 'I can't,' she whispered. 'Not yet.'

'No,' he agreed, and in that one word she could feel his compassion.

She watched him take the lid off his coffee and sip.

He looked up and caught her watching. 'Drink your coffee. At least it's hot.'

'Everyone seems to want me to drink something. The nurse back at the hospital kept wanting me to have tea.'

His smile was gentle. With fingers that trembled slightly she struggled with the plastic lid. Some of the hot liquid lurched over the side and scalded her fingers.

'Steady,' was all he said, reaching out to support her hand.

And then there was silence for a few moments before he began. His voice was quiet, deep and slightly husky.

'My wife, Eloise, was born with a defective heart. She should never... I should never have—'

Lucy waited. For the first time his pain pierced hers. This man knew exactly how she was feeling. He knew because he was in the same nightmarish place. Here with her. No one else would ever be able to understand how bleak it was possible to feel. But this man—Dominic—knew. He really knew.

He began again. 'Eloise always wanted children.' He looked down and traced a pattern with his shoe on the dry mud. 'But they never came. Month after month. There was nothing.'

Lucy sipped at the bitter coffee and waited as he struggled to get the words out. 'We didn't know about her heart then. Not then.' He looked up at the trees. 'Later we knew, of course, and we were told she shouldn't ever have a baby. There was a ''significant risk'', they told us. But Eloise was desperate. Her life wasn't ever going to be complete without children. I tried...'

She understood that desperation for a baby. Month after month of nothing. The feeling that somehow each month you'd lost your baby, even though your head told you there'd never been anything to lose. The sensation of life ebbing away, month after month. Lucy tried to think of something to say, some comfort.

'I let her go for the IVF. When Eloise knew she was pregnant she was so excited. Couldn't wait to have our baby.' He pulled himself up straighter on the bench. 'But there were complications during the Caesarean. She died giving birth to Abigail.'

Lucy hadn't expected that. Her right hand, holding the coffee, shook. *Died.* Her first reaction was one of sympathy, immediate and intense. 'I'm sorry. So sorry.'

'Abby is everything I have.'

His head was bowed and she could see the weight of everything resting on his shoulders. His wife had died giving birth to a child that wasn't his own—and yet he still loved his Abby. *Her Abby.* Just as she loved Chloe.

'How did you discover Abby—' her voice hovered over the unfamiliar name '—wasn't your natural child?'

'She has a rhesus—'

'Negative blood type. I remember. Dr Shorrock said.' She smiled sadly as he looked across at her. 'So do I.'

'I wish I'd never found out.' Dominic held her gaze. 'I love her more than anything in the world. She may not be my natural child but she's more mine than anyone—'

He broke off as though he'd suddenly re-membered whom he was speaking to. Yet Lucy didn't mind. She looked at the passion in his face and was glad Abigail had found some-where safe.

Safe. It was so strange. This stranger made her feel safe. Just sitting with him had begun to make the panic recede a little. The pain was still there. A hard knot at the very centre of who she was. And yet, looking at Dominic, she could believe she'd survive. That there might be a way to claw through this nightmare.

'I understand,' she said softly. 'I love Chloe.'

His eyes were moist as he breathed the name. 'Chloe. It's a beautiful name.'

'She's beautiful. An incredible little girl.' Lucy stood up and dropped the empty cup into the remains of a burnt-out litter bin. 'Shall we walk?'

'Yes.'

They took the path across the grass. 'Abigail's a lovely name too.'

'It means "father rejoiced". I wanted her to know I didn't blame her. When Eloise died,' he said awkwardly, and then he shrugged. 'It seemed important at the time.'

An understanding of just how much this man must have suffered washed over Lucy once again. His wife had *died* giving birth to Abigail.

Losing Michael had been painful, but she didn't have any sense of guilt about it. From the little he'd said it was obvious Dominic Grayling blamed himself, in part at least, for agreeing to the IVF treatment. Yet even in the midst of that tumult of emotion he'd still thought about his baby girl, how she would feel every birthday, and he'd given her a name that told her she was loved. He had to be a special kind of man.

'Is Abigail like me?' she asked, suddenly feeling the need to know. She turned to look at him, the wind whipping her hair across her face.

'A little. In the colour of her hair. But more, I think, in the way she moves. She moves like you.'

It was faintly embarrassing to have this stranger look at her in such a way. Focused. As though he could see nothing but her. Lucy looked away.

'And Chloe?'

'Yes,' she said hurriedly. 'She has your shape face, your hands...' *His hands.* She hadn't even registered she'd noticed his hands—and yet Chloe had the same long fingers. She'd always loved her daughter's fingers. Right from a baby. 'Artist's hands,' Michael had called them.

'I'd like to see her.'

He'd spoken quietly and yet the words were like a slap. Her head snapped up.

'No.'

'Don't you want to see Abigail?'

Lucy let his words flow over her.

'Can you really go your whole life without knowing what she's like?' He paused. 'Whether we like it or not, other people are going to start making decisions for us. When I first found out about Abby... Hell, this is hard.' He rubbed the back of his neck. 'My instinct was to keep it all quiet. Make sure no one discovered the mistake. Keep her mine. Just mine.' And his voice rang with possession.

Lucy met his eyes and the intensity in his kept her looking.

'But we can't do that. Either of us. Both girls have the right to know their genetic make-up. Chloe could perhaps need that more than Abby.'

A shiver of cold washed through her as she understood the implications of what he was trying to tell her. 'Is Eloise's heart condition hereditary?'

'It's possible for her to have inherited the same problem,' he stated baldly. 'But not likely.'

Lucy turned away as she felt the panic begin to rise up again. 'I can't bear this.'

'We have to.' Dominic caught her arm. 'Our girls are only six. Far too little to deal with this. We're the grown-ups here and we're going to have to deal with it.'

His fingers held her arm still, preventing her from walking away. She could almost imagine the warmth from his hand was giving her strength. Passing from him to her. She turned back towards him. 'I'm scared,' she whispered.

'If I could tell you everything's going to be all right I would. But I don't know that. I only know I'm going to do anything to protect Chloe and Abby from the consequences of this. I don't want to sue the hospital. I don't want any publicity.'

The mention of the word 'publicity' took the whole situation into another dimension. Lucy hadn't had time to think about the full ramifications of what had happened. She'd heard the defensive tone in Dr Shorrock's voice but it hadn't registered with her as anything other than awkwardness. But, yes, they could sue the hospital for negligence. But if they did, what then? A tragic mix-up at an IVF clinic would have all the elements needed to shoot the story to front-page prominence.

And then she thought of Chloe. A bright, sunny little girl who was already having to live her life without her daddy. Who had so few memories of the man who'd loved her for the first five years of her life.

'I don't want any publicity either.'

The tension in Dominic's face relaxed and he let go of her arm. 'I'm sure the courts will do everything they can to protect the girls. They're so young… I don't want to make this any more difficult for you and your family than it already is—but we can't pretend it hasn't happened either. I imagine we'll be asked to sign something that gives up all legal right to our biological children.'

Lucy frowned as she struggled to keep up with his conversation. He'd had longer to come to terms with the truth.

'But I'd like to see her,' he continued. 'Maybe have a photograph. A letter at Christmas. I can't make this situation right but I want my natural daughter to know I would have loved her. That I'll be there for her if ever she needs me.' His sincerity was tangible. 'And you must want that too. For Abby? Don't you?'

The little girl she didn't know? Abby? Yes, she wanted Abby to know she'd have loved her. 'Yes,' she said quietly. 'I do want that.'

'I think they're too young to be told everything. If you let me see Chloe occasionally you can be certain I'll never do anything to hurt her. I would just like to meet her. Talk to her for a little while so I can imagine her when I think about her.'

'And Abby?'

He nodded. 'I'd like her to know who you are. For you to be someone she likes so that when I have to tell her the truth she won't feel abandoned. I want her to know I did everything I could to make things right for her.'

Lucy looked back the way they'd walked un-seeingly. 'I'd like to see Abby.'

'Good.'

'And you can meet Chloe. But later. I can't do it now. Not now.'

His eyes softened and she felt the panic re-cede again. Dominic Grayling was a man to be trusted. The words popped into her head and they were comforting.

'First you must have Chloe checked out. Let's know what we are playing with.'

Lucy kept looking at his eyes, as though they were a life raft that was going to stop her being smashed against the jagged rocks. 'She was a very healthy baby.'

'That's good, then, isn't it? Let's just make sure.'

'I want to go home now.'

Dominic pulled a notepad from his pocket and finished filling out his name and address. 'Here,' he said, passing it across.

Dr Dominic Grayling. 'You're a doctor?'

'Not of medicine. I did a PhD. May I have your address?'

Lucy kept staring at the paper. 'Grayling. That's what Dr Shorrock meant. I hadn't real-ised before.' She looked back up at him. 'He said ''possibly there was some confusion over the names''. I'm Grayford.'

'Yes.'

She sighed. 'It doesn't seem possible, does it?' Taking his pen, she wrote swiftly. 'We live in Shropshire.'

Dominic accepted the notebook back. 'Will you be all right getting home? Is your husband in London with you?'

'Michael? No.' Lucy pulled her bag up on to her shoulder and pushed her hands down into the depths of her pockets. 'Oh, no, Michael's dead.'

'I'm sorry?'

'Michael died just before Chloe's fifth birthday.' She was really quite proud of the way she held her voice steady. 'I understand how you feel about Abby. I really do. Chloe's all I have too. I'm never going to let her go.'

CHAPTER TWO

LUCY glanced down at her watch and noticed with a jolt that it was already past seven. It was more than a jolt—she actually felt sick when she saw how late it was.

She'd meant to be so calm when she met Dominic again. She'd meant to be well groomed and in complete control but all her good intentions had turned to dust. Time had just flown by—in the way it always seemed to do when you knew there was something difficult ahead, she reflected as she searched out the small figure of her daughter in the middle of the play park. She was going to have to rush to be ready in time.

'Five minutes, Clo, and then we need to go to Grandma's,' she called out as she stood up to pack away their picnic things.

It was doubtful whether Chloe heard. Her feet were taking her in the direction of the giant slide, her blonde hair streaming out behind her. Lucy smiled. Nothing troubled Chloe's world and she was determined to keep it that way.

Whatever Dominic Grayling had to say this evening. Whatever any court of law had to say on the subject, she'd keep her safe and happy.

'Chloe, it's time to go. Five more minutes and that's it,' she called again.

Turning to reach for the picnic mat she stilled, suddenly aware of a solitary figure watching them. Perhaps her imagination had conjured him up? She was late, but not that late. He shouldn't be here. Not now. Dominic wouldn't do this without arranging it with her first. Would he? She had to be hallucinating, and yet…

With a fatalistic shrug the solitary figure started walking towards her until its identity became obvious.

'Hi,' Dominic said as he got close enough to speak.

His calm greeting fanned the tiny spark of anger into a fierce spurt. 'What are you doing here? You're more than an hour early.'

'Curiosity.'

'How dare you do this? You could be anyone, as far as Chloe's concerned. You could have scared her.'

'I'm sorry.'

But he didn't seem sorry. He seemed so relaxed, so completely in control, so...so what
she'd wanted to be when they'd met. 'What if
Chloe had noticed you watching her?'

'She didn't.'

'You can't know that.'

'I'm sure she didn't.' He turned to look at
her, his blue eyes narrowed astutely. 'Have I
scared you?'

His question caught her off guard. Was her
anger really all about her? How she felt? She
made a quick analysis of her feelings before
deciding on honesty. 'Yes.'

'I'm sorry.'

'For being here or for scaring me?'

But already her anger had dissipated. As a
disembodied voice on the telephone Dominic
Grayling still had charm, but in person it was
more evident. His hair was an indeterminate
sandy brown but his bone structure was strong
and characterful. A man to trust. A face to
paint, she thought inconsequentially. And of
course they shared a common bond in their
children. It was only natural she should feel a
connection to him. As his face relaxed into a
lopsided grin she felt the last shreds of her irritation pass—and yet surely that was illogical.

'I couldn't sit around at home any longer, and then the traffic from London was so clear I made much better time than I'd anticipated. I should have stopped at a service station and waited the time out, but I couldn't resist getting here earlier.'

Lucy hated the way she was letting him get away with spying on her. He should have walked down the hill and made sure she knew he was there instead of keeping his distance and watching. Better still, he should have stayed in London until it was really time to leave; he should have been held up on the motorway in a ten-mile traffic jam; he should have got lost at least a dozen times before he arrived at her house…

She turned her back. 'Do you want a coffee? There's some left in the flask.'

'I decided to walk about a bit. I didn't know you were here, Lucy.'

She turned back to him, hearing the coaxing, warm note to his voice. Sexy. *Where had that come from?* She didn't think like that about men any more. It was disloyal to Michael. It was too soon.

And Dominic Grayling wasn't sexy. He was, no doubt, a perfectly pleasant man, but he wasn't particularly special and he was a stranger to her. She had to remember that. She might feel she'd known him for months but the reality was different. 'So, as soon as you knew I was, you walked away?'

'Would you?' he asked on a slight smile.

She wouldn't, of course. The temptation to stand, unseen, to watch Abigail, would have been impossible to resist. To search for physical signs that would really make it possible to believe with her whole heart she belonged to her. Had it been like that for Dominic? Had he found them in Chloe?

'You're right; she's beautiful.'

Lucy hugged the picnic rug to her. 'Yes. Yes, she is.'

'She's got the same ash-blonde hair as Eloise.'

'Oh.'

He looked at her quickly. 'Was that the wrong thing to say?'

'Of course not. It's just…well, I'm sure you know,' she finished weakly, unaware of Chloe's small figure running up to join them.

'Are we going now?' Chloe asked, hesitating slightly as she joined them.

Lucy's fingers closed on her daughter's shoulder in a gesture she recognised as ownership. How was Dominic feeling now? Did this hurt? 'We have to.'

'Can't I stay five more minutes?'

'Not this time. We've got to get to Grandma's.' She hadn't dared to look up at Dominic but she sensed his stillness. This was an important moment for him—and for Chloe. Lucy took a deep, shaky breath. He didn't deserve to be ignored. However frightened she was by his presence in her life, by the whole situation. 'This is Dr Grayling. Do you remember me telling you about him?'

Chloe turned and looked with interest at the stranger. Whatever she saw she liked, because she suddenly smiled. It wasn't like her to do that. Chloe was always reserved and would rarely talk to adults she didn't know well. 'I'm Chloe.'

'I know. I've heard a lot about you from your mother.' Above her blonde head Dominic's eyes sought out Lucy's. It was part thanks, part reassurance. It was a reward in itself. She'd done the right thing and it felt really good.

'I'm going to sleep at my grandma's house tonight.'

Dominic smiled down at Chloe. 'I know. Your mummy told me.' It was the kind of half-smile that spoke of deep inner sadness. Lucy felt a sudden rush of compassion—for him, for her, for Chloe and Abby, for all the people who loved them. Her mum adored Chloe. She was her grandchild—and, of course, she was not. Somewhere Dominic would have a mother who'd been denied the right to know her own flesh-and-blood grandchild. The ramifications were endless. The ripples went on and on.

'Are you Mummy's new friend?' Chloe asked curiously.

Dominic didn't pause. 'Absolutely.'

'Come on, Chloe. Grandma will be waiting.' Lucy gratefully squeezed the hand tucked inside hers. The feel of those small fingers was so comforting.

And Dominic was alone. She could only imagine what he must feel like, watching them walk away from him. It must be the most hideous feeling. And it was going to be one she would experience when she met Abby.

Four weeks since her world had come crashing down for the second time and she'd not allowed herself to dwell on Abby. First there'd been the tests on Chloe's heart and the agonising wait before the all-clear had been given. Then there'd been contact with lawyers, the people who were going to determine the legal status of their children. And finally there was the desperate sense of being alone. More alone than she'd been when Michael died. Now she had to carry a deep, dark secret. One she could share with no one. Except Dominic. His telephone calls had been a lifeline. Calm, good sense in a crazy, shifting world.

'Am I staying for breakfast?' Chloe asked with a slight tug on her hand.

'Grandma would like you to.'

'Are you going to be there?'

Lucy smiled at the tone of her daughter's voice. If she said she was Chloe would be so disappointed. She wanted it to be just her and Grandma. 'No. I'll pick you up later.'

Chloe pulled back on her hand, looking behind her. 'Dr Grayling's still standing there. He hasn't moved.'

'Is he?'

'It's a bit rude to stare, isn't it?'

'Maybe he's lonely and wishes he could be coming home with us.'

Chloe thought about that carefully. 'He looked nice. We could both be friends with him.'

Could it really be as simple as that? Lucy wondered, her grip on Chloe's hand tightening. She wouldn't let anything hurt her. She'd take any painful blow if it would shield her from the consequences of this mess.

As they reached the corner Lucy risked a quick glance over her shoulder. Dominic was still standing there, watching, his hands thrust deep into his denim pockets and the lines of his body tense. He looked so alone.

And soon that would be her. Could she do it? It was impossible to imagine how that would actually feel. Would something in her recognise Abby as hers? Would she feel the same as she had when Chloe, newborn and angry at her difficult entry into the world, was placed in her arms? That overwhelming sense of love and responsibility. The total wonder at having created anything so perfect. That last thought twisted painfully inside her. *She* hadn't created Chloe. Given her life, yes, but not created. That was something she had to concede to Dominic and the fair-haired Eloise.

*   *   *

It was the hardest thing he'd ever done, Dominic decided as he watched the pair disappear. Light ash-blonde hair and a heart-shaped face. So like Eloise, and yet not.

Chloe was tanned, energetic and healthy. Her skin glowed with vitality and her eyes sparkled. Dressed in a faded T-shirt and old shorts, with tangled hair and a grubby face, she wasn't the image he'd held in his mind for the last few weeks. And yet this was better than all his imaginings. The euphoric feeling he'd experienced as he'd watched her balancing on the centre of the seesaw was something he'd never forget. She was happy.

Her little hand tucked safely in Lucy's was hard to see, but the bond between them was obvious. Chloe was loved and cared for. It was what he'd wanted to know and yet now it didn't feel like enough. He wanted his little girl to know about him. It was a spear of jealousy digging into his flesh.

He hadn't been able to stop thinking about her. And about Lucy. In his mind the two were intricately entwined. Lucy, so different from Eloise. His wife had been many wonderful things—cultured, intelligent, with the face of an angel—but he knew she'd have crumbled under this pressure. But Lucy would cope. Even in the immediate aftermath of hearing the news, shocked and desperately hurting, she'd still seemed strong. She had an inner core of strength that kept her standing. Whatever life threw at her, she would take it on the chin and move on. And it seemed life had thrown a good deal at her. Yet still she'd managed to raise a child who smiled as though her world was completely sunny.

A picnic in the park. He couldn't remember ever having taken Abby for a picnic. Since she'd started nursery her evenings had been filled with piano lessons, ballet classes and gymnastics. By the time he emerged from his study Abby was usually too tired to do anything but curl up against him for a story. What would Lucy make of that? She glowed with an active vitality that made him wonder whether she'd approve. Made him wonder whether he approved.

The doorbell rang at exactly eight-thirty. Even though she was expecting it, the sound still shocked her.

Lucy snapped on her wrist-watch and grabbed her handbag before opening the door.

'Do you always do this? You're exactly on time. To the minute.'

'I've been sitting outside in the car.'

'Oh,' she said, slightly deflated. It didn't seem right for him to have been doing that. She'd been so busy settling Chloe and hurrying back home to shower and change she hadn't thought about what Dominic was going to do with the spare hour. 'I suppose so. I'm sorry. I didn't think.'

'Is Chloe happily settled?'

'She loves staying with my mum. There's nothing so lovely as being spoiled, is there?' Lucy tried to say it with a laugh but it sounded more like a hiccup.

This felt so awkward. It had been easier on the telephone. Then she hadn't been confused by the tense, hurt look in Dominic's eyes. She'd only listened to his deep voice and the words he'd said. Calm and sensible, that was how she'd come to think of him. This felt different.

'Chloe said you looked nice,' she said on a rush, hoping it would make him feel better.

'She looks incredible. I don't know what I was expecting, but she looks so...so healthy.'

Lucy heard the wistful tone in his voice. Even that must be difficult for him, she remembered. Eloise had been anything but healthy, apparently. Did Chloe look like she would have done if she'd been well?

'I've booked a table at the White Horse since it's so near. I've no idea whether the food is any good, but I liked the idea of sitting on the terrace and watching the water.'

'The food's lovely,' Lucy volunteered quickly, glad he'd chosen that restaurant. She loved sitting where she could see water, watching the way the colour changed and shifted on the surface, but this time she liked the idea of having a distraction. Something easy to talk about if the conversation became too difficult, too strained.

They walked in silence for a time. Lucy was aware of the way he kept glancing down at her and she could feel the tension in his body. It didn't surprise her. What they were having to do was impossibly difficult.

'I used to go to the White Horse with Michael,' Lucy remarked, breaking the silence.

He seemed grateful. 'When you were dating?'

'No. We couldn't afford it then. Michael and I met at school and were married by the time we were nineteen. This is grown-up stuff, with grown-up prices. We went there for our last anniversary. A couple of months before he died.'

Dominic stopped and turned to look at her, the angled planes of his face pulled taut. 'Is this difficult for you? Look, if you'd rather go somewhere else please say so. This is awkward enough as it is.'

'It's fine, really. It's a happy place. I've really good memories of coming here.'

'Really?'

She nodded. 'Excellent.'

'What was he like?'

'Michael?' She saw the slight inclination of his head, saw his reluctance to ask the question in case it hurt her. Strangely, it didn't hurt to talk about Michael. What hurt was not being allowed to. Being widowed made other people uncomfortable, and sometimes it felt as if Michael had been erased. 'He was a lovely man. Very sporty, loved sailing. Always wanting to do the next thing, take on the next challenge. It was an incredible shock when he was diagnosed with the tumour. Of course he'd left it far too late. Wouldn't go to the doctor. He was the last person you'd ever have thought would...'

'I'm sorry. I shouldn't have asked.'

'No, it's fine. I like to talk about him sometimes,' she reassured him quickly. 'We were
really happy together. So many of my friends
are splitting up now, getting divorced. I know
I've already had more than some people have
their whole lives. If he hadn't died he wouldn't
have left me, and I know he loved me right up
to the end. Me and Chloe.'

'Do you find that difficult?' His shoe kicked
at a stone. 'That Michael died believing Chloe
was his natural child?'

Lucy watched it skim into the bramble
bushes. 'I'm glad about that. It's difficult for
me to cope with, but Michael would have found
it harder still. And if it had come when he was
ill… That would have been unbearable. As it is
he died happy, knowing I wouldn't be alone
and believing something of him was going on.'
She swallowed painfully. 'And it still is. Except
in your Abby—not in Chloe, as we thought.'

Dominic held open the gate for Lucy to pass
through before him, thinking once again how
remarkable a woman she was. How did you
reach the point where you could be glad for the
little time you'd had? Every time he caught
sight of an article celebrating someone's diamond wedding anniversary he felt angry. Every

time he saw a mother with her child he remembered Eloise hadn't had that chance. Was it possible Lucy didn't share his anger—and guilt?

He waited until they were seated at one of the tables overlooking the canal before he spoke again. 'Have you ever been on the canal?'

Lucy tucked her handbag beneath her seat and looked up to see a burgundy-and-blue narrow boat passing, small crochet circles hanging in the round windows. 'Absolutely. I grew up near here. My mum and dad owned a narrow boat for most of my childhood. They had a seventy-two foot boat which they called *Little Beauty*.'

'An odd choice for a big boat.'

Lucy smiled and his breath caught in his throat. Her skin seemed to glow with pure life, even her hair crackled with energy. The first time he'd seen her, outside the hospital, he'd recognised she was a beautiful woman but he hadn't anticipated his reaction to her smile. He'd no business thinking about her that way. Even so, when she smiled she took on a luminosity that was quite staggering. Her expressive eyes sparkled and her soft full mouth... What? He caught himself up on the thought.

'*Little Beauty* is such a ridiculous name. I was always embarrassed by it until I read H E Bates.'

He frowned, trying to pick up the threads of her conversation.

'*Darling Buds of May*. *Little Beauty* is the boat owned by Pop Larkin. Once I knew that, I loved it. The biggest mystery is my dad going along with it. He wasn't that kind of man.'

'Wasn't?' Dominic prompted.

'He died when I was twenty-three. He was a very careful man. *Little Beauty* was his only extravagance. He believed life was too difficult to be reckless with it. He was so worried when I went to art college.'

So there was the answer to one of the questions he'd wanted to ask her. She was an artist. That fitted her image perfectly. With her dark hair pulled up on the top of her head in a haphazard manner, long wispy tendrils curling around her face, she looked slightly bohemian. Messy.

'What about you? What do you do, Dr Grayling? What are you a doctor of?'

He smiled. He'd suspected she'd no idea who he was. It was refreshing. It was difficult to live down the description of being the 'thinking woman's crumpet', and London was full of women who liked the idea of being with a man who made intellectual television programmes. It had led to hours of spurious conversations with people who'd no idea what they were talking about but who hoped to impress him with their knowledge.

'History.'

'Revolting. A truly horrible subject. There were far too many essays to write in History—and almost all of them were about war, I seem to remember.'

His smile broadened. 'You obviously had some appalling teachers.'

'So what does a doctor of History actually do?'

'I'm more of a writer now, but history is still an overwhelming passion,' he answered evasively, not really understanding his strange reluctance to tell her what he actually did. 'I see myself as an educator.' He broke off as the waitress arrived at their table. 'Are you ready to order? Have you had time to decide what you'd like?'

'No debate. Scampi and chips,' she answered with determined cheerfulness. 'I'll worry about the calories tomorrow.'

That made a change, Dominic thought. Both his wife and his mother would never have let a sentiment like that enter their heads, let alone passed their lips. Rigid control at all times. He'd even come to believe they actually preferred lettuce and steamed broccoli.

'If it comes that highly recommended I'll have the same. What would you like to drink?'

'I'll have a glass of dry white wine, please.'

The waitress scribbled frantically. 'House white?'

'Will be lovely,' Lucy replied with a wide smile.

Without it being a conscious decision, Dominic was watching her closely. Searching for a fault, some reason why he shouldn't go through with the idea that had been sitting in his brain since the first day they'd met.

Lucy seemed to be oblivious.

'Have you lived in London for long?'

Dominic sat back in his chair. 'Since I finished my PhD. Yes.'

'And before then?'

'Oxford—and before that I was at boarding school.'

Lucy smiled. 'Oxford! Now I know where Chloe gets her brains from.'

The waitress returned with their drinks. Lucy shifted slightly to make it easier for her to put the glass down.

'Is she bright?'

'Very. Top of her class in practically everything. She's just been selected for a gifted and able programme. She's going to work with older children on a computer project.'

The feeling of satisfaction spread through him.

'What's Abby like?'

Dominic picked up his beer and took a small sip. 'She's bright. Top sets. But her passion is for art. She really loves that. 3D art, though, more than drawing.'

As he said it he realised he'd done very little to encourage that in Abby. Her evenings were so full of activities, and yet none of them really addressed what she loved to do. He'd allowed his in-laws to take far too much responsibility in Abby's upbringing and they were reproducing what they'd done for Eloise. It would have suited her, but Abby was different. She'd love to be given a lump of clay, or just be encouraged to make a mess with papier-mâché.

'Art? I don't believe it!'

Lucy's face shone with a radiance he was coming to expect. She was so easy to read. When she was pleased everything of it showed on her face. She couldn't hide anything. 'So much for nature versus nurture, then.'

With no regard for their conversation, the scampi was brought to the table. The plates were steaming hot and generously full.

'I'm so hungry,' Lucy remarked, spearing a chip with her fork.

This place suited her, with its casual informality. At home he would have chosen a select little bistro, where everything would have been arranged in delectable morsels. Lucy was like a breath of fresh air. She sat in tight, hip-hugging black trousers and a white broderie anglaise top and looked as if someone had just ruffled her in a haystack. Effortlessly sexy. It made him remember sensations and feelings he'd tried hard to bury for the past few years.

'Do you paint still?'

'Occasionally. I found it difficult to do when Michael was ill. I couldn't seem to concentrate enough. My mum's a potter, and I've spent more time recently working with her. It's nice to have company and have the feel of the clay between my fingers.' She took a sip of wine.

'Chloe's done some lovely things. I ought to show you some time.'

He felt a sudden spear of guilt. Abby had never had the opportunity to do anything like that. He should have been more assertive. Whatever the outcome of this evening, he was going to make some changes.

'I'd like that.'

Lucy bit into a piece of scampi before looking up at him. Her face was suddenly serious. 'I'm sorry about earlier. It felt really strange, seeing you watching Chloe like that. It was just I wasn't expecting to see you then. You know—wrong place, wrong time.'

'Nothing about this situation is easy.' Dominic played for time by picking up his pint glass. 'Have you thought about what might happen when our case goes to court?'

Her eyes widened slightly in alarm. 'I thought everyone was fairly confident. We'll each have legal guardianship—'

'Yes. And be recognised as the natural birth parent of each other's children. But nothing like this has ever gone to court before.'

'It has. I was told—'

Dominic cut her off again. 'This case is slightly different. We had a direct swap of embryos.'

'What do you think will happen?' Lucy asked, putting down her fork carefully.

'I don't know—and I don't like it. I hate having no control over what other people are deciding about my life.'

Her face was a picture of worry, her dark eyes clouded with anxiety, and her hand went up to pull nervously at her hair. He didn't like to do this to her but she needed to know. He had to make sure she understood exactly what they were facing.

'What do you hope happens?'

Dominic shook his head. 'It's an impossible question to answer. At first I just wanted to go on with Abby as before. Then I wanted to keep Abby but maybe hear about my natural daughter. Not too often. Just once in a while. Enough to know she was all right.'

'And now?'

'Now I want it all.'

Lucy shifted in her chair, her face uncharacteristically pale. 'You want both girls?'

'In a way. I—'

'You can't do that—'

'Hear me out, Lucy. I'm not suggesting I sue for custody.'

She shook her head, obviously bemused. 'Then what?'

This was it then. An irrevocable decision. Once made there could be no going back. Dominic leant forward. 'I want you to marry me.'

The silence echoed around the table. For a moment Lucy wondered whether she'd heard him correctly. *It wasn't possible, was it?* His eyes were watching her steadily, waiting for an answer. Colour flooded into her ashen face.

'But I don't know you!'

His voice remained steady. 'I don't know you either. Except through Abby. I want Abby to have everything—and that means you.'

For the girls. He wanted to marry her for the girls. Lucy held her bottom lip between her teeth, her stomach twisting and turning. What he was suggesting was outrageous. How could you marry someone you didn't know and knew nothing about?

His voice continued inexorably. 'When I think about a future hearing just snippets about Chloe I can't bear it. I want it all.' He paused.

'And the obvious way to achieve that is a marriage of convenience.'

Lucy looked at him in complete horror. She felt as if the floor had just disappeared beneath her and she was falling down into an alternative reality. *This couldn't be happening.*

He'd been her rock. Since she'd first discovered the mix-up Dominic had been what had kept her standing. He'd understood how she was feeling, understood the unmitigated agony of living with the secret knowledge that your child wasn't really yours. She felt slightly betrayed. Angry.

'Real people don't do things like that.'

'Think about it. We could be there for the girls. For as long as they need us. While the courts argue about how much contact the birth parents should have we can solve it all in one clean sweep. They can have us both.'

He made it sound so reasonable—and yet it wasn't. *It wasn't.* She wanted everything to be right for the girls. Wanted to make life perfect for Chloe. To know Abby was happy. *But marriage?* How could he suggest spending the rest of his life with someone he'd only met for the second time today?

Her fingers played nervously with the edge of the starched white tablecloth. What did he mean by a 'marriage of convenience' anyway? Did he imagine he'd share her bed?

'Marriage?'

'In name only.'

He could see the questions whizzing across her face. If it hadn't been so serious he would have found it funny. He watched the moment arrive when she decided there was one question she really had to ask.

'No sex?'

'Absolutely. What I want is a mother for Abby, and I want to be a father for Chloe. This is about parenting.'

She went to pick up her wine glass and then stopped. 'Why marriage?'

'Because it's a sign of commitment. Then I can formally adopt Chloe and you can adopt Abby. If the court allows it. Personally, I think they're going to breathe a sigh of relief that everything's worked out so smoothly.'

This time she did take a sip of wine. He watched the nervous flutter of her hand as she replaced the glass carefully back on the table. At least she hadn't said an outright no.

'You want to be married until the girls are eighteen?'

He shook his head. 'As long as they need us to be. It has to be as normal as we can make it. At some point in the future we're going to have to tell them the complete truth, and I want them to be secure in having two parents who love them and are there for them.'

Again the questions flitted across her expressive face. Her hand went to her casually swept-up hair and fiddled with a strand hanging across her cheek. 'What happens if you meet someone else? Or I do?'

'It hasn't happened to me in the last six years. I hardly think it's likely to happen now. I don't ever want to love anyone again. I can't take the risk of anything hurting that much again.' He had her attention now. It was in the way she leant forward and her hand stilled on her hair. 'We have a common goal. It will be enough to build a good life for ourselves—and for the girls.'

'And where will we live?'

Was that a yes? He'd shocked her, unquestionably, but she could obviously see the advantages of a marriage of convenience. 'If we decide to go ahead with it, that's all open for discussion. It's handy for me to be based in London, and I've a big house there, so that's an option, but it's not a necessity. Are you fixed here?'

'My family's here. Friends.'

Memories, he realised, watching the way she bit on her bottom lip. 'The details can be worked out later. In principle, what do you think? Will you marry me?'

Lucy didn't know what to say. What to think, even. Could she do it? Marry a perfect stranger? To give Chloe security and get to know Abby? And then she gave a half smile. *Perfect?* Had she really thought that? He *was* perfect—almost. Tall, handsome—in a clever kind of way, rather than a chocolate box model kind of thing. Gorgeous hands, eyes you could trust, and a committed father as well. It was an impressive list. But he didn't love her and she didn't love him.

It was a big but. If she'd been young and impressionable he'd have been someone she might have dated—if it hadn't been for Michael. There never had been anyone for her but Michael and never would be. People only had one great love in a lifetime and she'd already had hers. It had been fantastic—and now it was over.

All she had in her life were memories—and Chloe. Lucy looked out at a small family cruiser passing outside on the canal. A mum, a dad and two little girls. She bit her lip. She could do that for Chloe. For Abby. If there was no possibility of her falling in love again she could commit herself to this new family unit. The girls could have everything. She looked back at Dominic.

'I'll do it. Theoretically, if we can work it all out, I'll do it. For the girls, I'll marry you.'

She couldn't believe she'd said the words that would commit her to a lifetime without love. It seemed a travesty of everything she'd shared with Michael. He wouldn't have wanted her to spend the rest of her life alone in every way that mattered. Yet Michael couldn't have known what would face her.

Dominic leant forward. 'We can make this work, Lucy. I know we can.'

She could feel her eyes begin to fill up with tears and she blinked furiously. When she'd agreed to have dinner with Dominic to discuss the future she hadn't dreamed the conversation would take this turn. It certainly wasn't some-

thing that usually happened to a widowed
mother of one who only wanted a peaceful life.
'What do we do now?'

Watching Dominic, she noticed a change.
The tension had left him and in its place was a
sense of purpose. She had the strangest sensation of being in a bubble. Everything was muffled, it was slower, it was…inevitable.

'Are you working at the moment? Apart from
on a casual basis with your mother?' She knew
she'd shaken her head when she heard him say,
'That simplifies things.'

Did it? Nothing seemed very simple to her.
She could see every obstacle. She knew nothing
about him. Not even what he did for a job, she
recognised bleakly. Some kind of lecturer, perhaps? It hardly mattered.

'We could start off in London and review it
later. My house has room for some kind of a
studio for you. I don't know what you need for
potting, but there's an annexe on the ground
floor that was intended for live-in help. It could
be made into something quite useful. We could
put in a wheel. A kiln? Is that what you need?'

Everything was moving too fast. He was answering questions she hadn't even got around
to thinking yet. Was he really asking whether

she wanted her own studio? It was unbelievable. She couldn't get her head round it at all. This just couldn't be happening to her.

'Mum mainly produces named mugs for the tourist market. I'd rather try and paint again.' This was just surreal. 'And I like to teach. I've been doing a bit at the local secondary school while their art teacher has been off on maternity leave. I could do more of that.'

'There's a desperate shortage of teachers in London, so I can't see that as a problem.' He filled up his fork and ate another mouthful. 'What we ought to do now is get on with organising our wedding. There's no point in hanging about now we've made the decision. I'm assuming we'll go for a civil ceremony.' He frowned. 'I think the rules have changed since the last time I got married. I think there's a month's delay from visiting the register office to the wedding itself.'

'Is there?' Lucy heard herself ask.

'Minimum. I suggest you move in with Abby and I as soon as possible and we'll set everything in motion. If the wedding is, let's say, eight weeks from now, it gives us some time to review it.'

'Review it?' she repeated weakly.

'Once we're married there can be no turning back. We'll be in it for the long run. For better, for worse and all that.'

CHAPTER THREE

TAKING off the wedding ring Michael had given her was the difficult bit, Lucy thought. It really felt like the end of one life and the beginning of another. She looked down at her left hand as it rested on the steering wheel, at the white band indelibly printed on her skin, marking where her ring used to be. Practically all her adult life she'd worn Michael's ring and now it really was over.

She was driving towards a new life. A new daughter.

'Are we nearly there yet?' Chloe asked, lifting her head from the awkward angle it had fallen to while she had slept.

'Very close now, sweetheart.'

They had left the motorway and were weaving through closely populated suburban housing. It was dirtier and greyer. *And this was her new life?* There were no fields dotted with cows, no picture-book cottages, no meandering little streams cutting between the hills. In their place were manmade recreational spaces and row upon row of post-war housing.

'How much longer?'

A bus moved up on the lane beside her. 'It's not far. Let me concentrate for a minute. There's a turning off to the left somewhere near here.'

She'd always hated the idea of city life. The city had always seemed to her to be a grubby place to live. Some people saw opportunity, but all she saw was the claustrophobia of it all. Yet this was what she'd chosen. For the good of Chloe—and Abby, whom she'd never met—she was going to make her life here.

The road whipped round and the houses became more spaced out, some even attractive.

It was a strange feeling. Almost like the first day in a new job. A mixture of excitement, anticipation and pure fear. Since the moment she'd opened her eyes that morning a feeling of nausea had settled deep in her stomach.

Within the next few minutes she was going to meet the little girl she and Michael had created together. But for an administrative error it would have been this little girl she'd spent the last six years loving. Would she feel anything for her? Would it be enough to sustain her, spending her future with a man who didn't love her and who openly admitted he didn't want to?

She rounded another bend and turned into a wide, tree-lined avenue. 'This is it,' Lucy announced in complete disbelief.

'We're going to stay *here*?'

Lucy looked down at the awe in Chloe's face. It was an emotion she shared. She reached into the side pocket of her car door and pulled out the sheet of paper she'd written his directions on before turning to look back at the huge picture windows and curved brickwork of Dominic's home. In her wildest imaginings she'd not conjured up anything like this.

She took a deep, shaking breath. 'For a while. Come on, let's go and meet Abby.'

She turned the car up the wide drive and brought it to a halt outside the imposing front entrance. *She'd never fit in here. Never.* She hadn't given Dominic's financial status much thought. Her mind had been too preoccupied with everything else. But, faced with this huge chasm between them, she wished she had. What did the blasted man do anyway, to make this kind of money? She should have noticed the T-shirt he'd worn was expensive, that the fabric was thick and didn't look as if it had been through the washing machine a couple of hundred times.

For the first time she felt conscious of her own clothes. There were no designer labels in her wardrobe, just simple cottons and natural wool jumpers she put together in a style she hoped was entirely her own. She probably didn't present the understated elegance he was used to. If it had been possible to turn round and run she would have done so. Instead, she helped Chloe from the car and firmly shut the door.

A small face was watching from the window, and it made her heart pound as she caught a glimpse of dark hair before it darted away. With Chloe's hand held tightly in hers, she walked unsteadily up the three wide steps. *Please, oh, God, please let Abby like me*, she prayed under her breath.

'They're here. They're here!' she heard as the door swung open and a small dark-haired figure darted out underneath Dominic's arm. 'You're late!' Abby stopped before Chloe. 'You've been ages getting here. We've had your bedroom ready for hours. You're in the blue room, next to mine. It's a nice blue and it's got yellow flowers on the bed. Do you like dolls? I don't.'

Abby didn't seem to need to draw breath. It was like being greeted by a whoosh of water, even though all her remarks were directed at Chloe. With the complete ease of childhood the two girls decided they were friends and, with tacit agreement, Abby rushed Chloe into the house and up the stairs, their voices becoming muffled.

'I'm sorry,' Dominic said, walking towards Lucy and guiding her more gently through the front door. 'Abby's been up for hours and is very excited.'

She looked at him through a mist of tears. *That was Abby.* A mini-volcano of energy. 'Just like that,' she said with a shaky smile. 'We put them together and they act like best friends. Chloe isn't normally like that. She takes a while to warm up to people. I can't believe she went upstairs like that.'

Dominic's face lit into his lopsided grin. 'Abby is exactly like that, I'm afraid.' He shut the door behind her. 'You'll get a chance to meet her later, when she's calmed down a bit. Right now she can't see past having a friend to stay. I suppose she's a bit lonely.'

'It's fine, really.' And it was fine, she realised as she heard laughter from upstairs. All this was about the girls, and if they were happy then she was too. 'There'll be plenty of time to get to know her later.'

And him. There was going to be plenty of time to get to know him. Years and years, if everything went to plan. A sterile façade of a marriage. Would the girls be enough to see her through those years of her life, or would she wake up one day and realise she wanted more?

'Right,' he said, his tone over-bright. 'I suppose I ought to get you a drink. Does Chloe need anything after her journey?'

Lucy twisted the strap on her handbag. 'I'm sure she's fine. We stopped off for a break just before we hit London.'

'Right.'

The silence stretched between them, awkward and cavernous. 'This is an amazing house.'

'Thank you.'

'I didn't imagine you living somewhere like this. I suppose I thought a historian would prefer something old.'

Dominic's eyes relaxed into a smile. 'With cannons perched on all the turrets? I'm afraid you're going to be disappointed. Let me show you around.' He pushed open the door to the left. 'This is the main living room. We don't tend to use it very often.'

Lucy could see why. It was a beautifully proportioned room, with high ceilings and plenty of light, but it was like something from a magazine advertisement. It made a strong statement, with bold, clear lines and dramatic accent colours, but it was a room without personality. It was a tasteful design statement, but she knew no more about the man she'd promised to marry from seeing this room than she had before.

What she was certain of was that she was unlikely to use the room much herself either. She could no more imagine herself curling up in one of the sofas with a good book and a glass of wine than running stark naked through Oxford Street singing 'We Wish You a Merry Christmas'.

'Through here,' Dominic continued as he led the way through double doors, 'is a dining room. It's useful for entertaining.'

The room was decorated in a similar palette of neutral shades, with the same slashes of aubergine. 'Do you entertain often?' she asked, feeling slightly nervous. Anyone who expected to be entertained in this kind of style wasn't going to be her type of person at all. No one she knew would expect anything other than a spicy casserole, washed down with plenty of cheap wine and eaten round the kitchen table.

'Not often,' he said, unaware of the relief his words sent coursing through her before he dashed them. 'Probably once a month, on average.'

'Is that for business or pleasure?'

He hesitated before answering. 'Work and home overlap. I'd say it was both.'

Worse and worse, Lucy thought. If he imagined she'd ever be able to act as a hostess to the kind of dinner party this room demanded he was going to be very disappointed. 'What's through there?' she asked, pointing to another set of double doors leading off the sitting room.

'The conservatory. It goes along the entire back of the house. Through here—' Dominic opened the single door nearest to them '—is the kitchen. The conservatory leads off this too.'

The kitchen was hideous. Of all the rooms she'd seen so far it was the one she hated most intensely. The overwhelming impression was of functional steel. How anyone with a child could live in such a house was beyond her. Her own kitchen was painted in warm colours and the cheap pine cupboards were disguised with a clever paint effect. Chloe's pictures and swimming certificates decorated the walls and it felt homely. This could have been something in a restaurant for all the personality it showed.

'It's very well designed,' she said carefully.

Dominic smiled, pausing to study her face. 'Do you hate it?'

'It's a little overwhelming.'

He walked over to the stainless steel kettle and filled it with water from the tap. 'It was designed by Joseph Finchingly.'

'Oh.' Was she supposed to know who he was? If so she was failing miserably, because she'd never heard of him.

'Eloise, my wife, was in the same year at Oxford as his son. When the opportunity came to build something for ourselves he was the obvious choice.' He set the kettle on to boil. 'The house is a complete concept. He designed everything and even chose the furniture.'

She might have guessed the person who had to live in it hadn't designed it. 'Isn't it hard to keep clean? Doesn't all this stainless steel show every fingerprint?'

He looked at her blankly, as though the question had never occurred to him before. 'Jessie deals with all that.'

'Jessie?'

'Jessica Monroe. Haven't I mentioned her? Jessie arrived on a short-term contract shortly after Abby was born and stayed on. I'll introduce you to her tomorrow. She sees to all the cleaning, and much of the day-to-day cooking, but she's more like family now.'

Lucy twisted the strap on her shoulder bag nervously. 'Will she mind me suddenly arriving on her patch?'

'Why should she? You won't want to be bothered with the house if you're painting, will you? While the kettle's boiling I'll show you the annexe I thought you could use as a studio.'

Lucy followed him out of the kitchen, through another door and across a small inner hallway. The place was like a rabbit warren. Everything led into everything else. All of it painted in shades of white and off-white, with dramatic pictures and minimal furnishings. Surely it was an unusual home for a man who loved history? She'd imagined him surrounded by books in rooms of deep burgundy and green, not living in this monument to minimalism.

What kind of man was Dominic Grayling really?

'This is the annexe,' he said, standing back.

Dominic appeared almost anxious as he looked at her for her reaction. Did he honestly think her being here depended on whether this space was suitable for a studio? From what she'd seen of the house so far she wasn't holding her breath.

Stepping down into the room, Lucy looked around in surprised delight. It was a completely empty space, with huge French windows leading directly out into the garden. 'This is fantastic.'

'Through here is a small kitchenette, and this door leads to a bedroom. Will it do, do you think?'

It was touching to see how much he seemed to want her to like this room. Had he guessed how much she disliked the rest of the house? 'It would make an amazing studio. Why aren't you using it for anything else?'

He shut the door to the bedroom and turned back to her. 'Jessie used to live here when Abby was a baby. A couple of years ago she married Steven, very unexpectedly.' He smiled. 'She's mid-forties and was always adamant she'd never marry. She said she liked to "cook and clean for a man" but that's where her duties stopped.'

Lucy walked towards the French doors. She saw a small but perfectly formed oasis of calm. 'What's behind the trees?'

'A swimming pool. I keep it locked because of Abby, but obviously if you want to take the girls there...' He trailed off and looked at her. 'What are you thinking?'

'That I'm a bit out of my depth here.'

He took a few steps towards her and gently turned her round to face him. 'We can do this. I know we can. It's bound to feel awkward in the beginning but it will get easier.'

The feel of his fingers on her arms was beginning to do strange things to her tummy—a nervous flutter of...what? Awareness? Attraction? Lucy took an involuntary step backwards. She couldn't begin to feel anything for Dominic Grayling. That wasn't part of the plan. She rushed into speaking. 'It just feels strange. You know, to be moving in with someone I hardly know.'

'It'll get easier,' Dominic reiterated, moving away. 'What we've got to do is make sure we're completely honest with each other. If we have a problem we must talk about it.'

Lucy nodded. Words like that sounded reasonable, but they weren't when you actually thought it through. How likely was it she'd ever say, When you touched me just then I suddenly noticed how attractive you are? Even if he hadn't made it totally plain he didn't want that from her she still wouldn't. Anything of that kind would just complicate everything beyond belief.

She moved back towards the French doors. If they were really going to do this she was going to need a bolt-hole, a place she could hide herself away. Maybe the annexe was the answer. 'Can I really use this space for anything?'

'Of course.'

'Make it mine? Put my own stamp on it?'

'Go ahead,' he replied. 'I'd better go back to the kettle. Do you want tea? Coffee?'

'Tea. Thanks,' Lucy said, following him back out. 'What have you said to people about my coming here?'

'Not a great deal.'

'To Abby?' she asked, leaning on the doorframe and watching the way he deftly made the tea. He might leave most things domestic to the absent Jessie but he knew his way around his own kitchen. Michael hadn't. But then she was beginning to expect Dominic to be good at everything he did.

'I told Abby you were a special friend and I wanted her to meet you. What have you told Chloe?' he asked, handing her a large cream mug.

'Much the same. I said you'd a daughter the same age as her and we wanted to know if they could be friends.' Lucy wrapped her hands around the mug. 'Obviously I had to say a bit more to my mum. I told her we were thinking about getting married but we needed to see how the girls got on. She couldn't quite believe it.'

'Not surprising, really. How long is it exactly since Michael died?'

'It'll be two years at Christmas,' Lucy answered, hiding her face by sipping more tea.

There was a momentary reprieve as the sound of running feet echoed down the wooden floor of the hallway. Within seconds, Abby had burst in. 'Dad, can I show Chloe the garden? She says she doesn't have a climbing frame at her house because there isn't room.'

Dominic moved to open the doors of the conservatory at the far end of the kitchen. 'Go on, then.'

Chloe hovered nervously in the doorway. Lucy smiled encouragingly at her. 'Is everything okay?'

'This house is enormous,' she whispered.

'Isn't it?' Lucy replied conspiratorially.

'I've got a dressing table in my bedroom.'

'Come on, Chloe,' Abby interrupted. 'I want to show you the climbing frame. It's got a swing part on it too.'

With the same bustling energy she'd shown the last time, Abby swept the quieter Chloe out through the door and through the trees to the hidden part of the garden.

'They seem to be getting on all right,' Dominic remarked, turning back to her. 'Come and sit in the conservatory. We can see them coming back from there and I'd rather they didn't overhear our conversation.'

Lucy sat nervously in one of the armchairs. 'Are we right to be doing this? Keeping it all a secret from them?'

'They're too young, and both of them have already lost one parent. I don't see we've much choice.'

'It feels like I'm lying, though,' she said, her fingers twisting together.

Dominic leant forward and touched her hand. 'When they're older we'll tell them everything, and by then they'll be secure in knowing they're loved by us both.'

She looked down at their linked fingers and felt comforted. They were in this together. Just the two of them. 'And you still think we shouldn't tell our families?'

The shake of his head was decisive. 'The fewer people who know, the less chance there'll be of the girls being told anything before we think they're ready. Besides, how confident are you in your mother, for example, being able to treat Chloe in exactly the same way as before? You must have had your reasons for not confiding in her when you had that first appointment with Dr Shorrock.' Lucy shifted uncomfortably in her chair. It was confirmation enough for him and he continued, 'Knowledge can be difficult to deal with.'

He was right. She wasn't entirely sure of her reasons for keeping everything to herself, but she'd asked her mum to look after Chloe without telling her why she needed to go to London. She met his eyes, acutely aware of her hand resting in his. She felt as if anything she said now would be as sacrosanct as something said in a confessional. 'Mum's hurt because I didn't tell her about you. She thinks you're the reason I've been coming up to London so much recently.'

The grip on her fingers tightened in sympathy before he let her go. 'There's no rule book for how we deal with all of this. We're going to have to find our way through it as best we can.' Dominic sat back in his chair. 'You ought to be warned that Jessie's imagining a great romance.'

'Won't that be awkward?'

'We're hardly teenagers any more. She won't expect us to be kissing in corners, and for the next month or so she'll be happy with the idea we're having separate bedrooms because of the girls. After the wedding...' He hesitated. 'Well, that's just another thing we'll have to work out when we get there.'

Lucy took a sharp intake of breath. The images filling her head of what it would be like to share a room with Dominic were entirely inappropriate. She could only hope he didn't have any idea of what was running through her mind. 'I suppose so,' she managed. 'Perhaps we could tell her we need separate rooms because I like to paint at night.'

'Do you?'

'No—but we could say I do.'

She could hardly breathe, the air was so charged between them. If he hadn't told her he didn't want any real connection between them she could have imagined he was as aware of her as she was becoming of him. His eyes didn't leave her face. It made her uncomfortable, and the words she wanted to say felt as if they were getting jumbled in her head.

'I know,' she continued a little desperately. 'I could use the bedroom in the annexe. We could say I sleep down there if I've been doing a lot of late-night painting. I'm always up early anyway...'

'Sounds like a good idea. Jessica wouldn't suspect anything if you kept most of your things in the dressing room off my bedroom.'

'Fine.' She drank the last of her tea in a gulp. 'That'll work really well.'

Ahead of her were years and years of trying to fool people...the girls...everyone...that they had a normal marriage. It was a depressing thought.

'I've told Eloise's parents you're coming to stay.'

Lucy put her mug down on the low rosewood table. 'And what did they say?'

'Obviously they find the idea of my marrying again quite difficult.'

'You told them we're getting married?'

'Thinking about it,' he corrected. 'I've had some girlfriends since Eloise died, but nothing serious. Nothing that involved them or Abby. Until now.'

Dominic sat back in his chair. Why had he started this conversation? Lucy was tense enough already, without having the added pressure of knowing just how difficult his parents-in-law were finding the mere idea he might replace their daughter in his life. He wasn't sure whether their objections were because they finally had to accept Eloise had died or because they knew another woman in the house would erode the control they had over Abby's upbringing.

'It's difficult for them. They adored Eloise.'

'Obviously.'

'How about you? Your in-laws?'

She jumped nervously, and he cursed himself for the insensitive question, but she answered anyway. 'I haven't told them anything yet. I don't think they'll mind, though. Michael was one of six children and his parents live in Scotland now, near one of their daughters. I'm sure they'll just be pleased Chloe and I are doing all right without him. As long as they still get to see her sometimes...' She faltered.

'Have you dated since he died?' It was probably an extremely crass question, but he wanted to know the answer.

'No.'

'It's still quite recent for you, isn't it?' he acknowledged quickly, taking pity on her tightly clasped hands. He was probably wrong to be rushing her into this marriage, but he couldn't see any alternative. He changed tack abruptly, to refocus on exactly why they were in this invidious position. 'Have you heard from Dr Shorrock in the past couple of days?'

'I telephoned him to say he could contact me here. I'm not sure he thinks what we're doing is wise.'

Dominic almost snorted in irritation. 'I don't think he's in any position to make any comment about it.'

'He wasn't responsible for the mistake,' she countered, looking up at him. 'He says it will take several months before our case goes to court, and he advises us to wait for the ruling before we make any irrevocable decisions.'

'Does he? No one outside of us can have any idea what this actually feels like.'

'Which is what I said to him,' Lucy said quietly, unclasping her hands. 'I do believe he's genuinely concerned for us, though. And for the girls.'

'I wish I did. I get the feeling they're all fascinated by this interesting ethical dilemma. The lawyers have a case they can really get their teeth into. They've got rulings on embryos created when the egg was fertilised by the wrong sperm and then implanted, but they've got nothing where the birth mother isn't genetically connected to the baby at all.

'Apparently there was a triple mix-up a while back, but it was discovered after a few hours and they made sure no pregnancies resulted. We're on our own in this one. Let them talk about it, make their rulings and do their investigations, but let's make a good future for ourselves. For the girls.'

She nodded and smiled. Although it wavered slightly it was still a smile. She brushed her hair away from her face. 'I told him the ruling wouldn't make any difference to our decision. Nothing they say will change the love I feel for Chloe or the fact Abby's my biological child. Their mistake has left us with few choices.'

'What did he say to that?'

She shrugged. 'What was there to say? He just assured us of his support. Told me everything's progressing much as he expected and he'd be in contact shortly.'

For the umpteenth time he was touched by her bravery. Unquestionably frightened and hurting, she'd moved herself and her daughter to live with an unknown man in a strange city. That took some courage and he admired her for it.

'I suggest we don't leave too much time before telling the girls we're thinking of getting married. Let's give them as much time to get used to the idea of being sisters as possible.'

He broke off to listen as the sound of giggles outside grew louder. With little warning, two figures streaked across the lawn towards the conservatory. Lucy suddenly found it difficult to swallow as she struggled not to cry. Seeing Abby—seeing the two of them together—was incredibly moving.

She'd wondered how she would feel when she looked at Abby. She hadn't believed it possible she'd be able to love anyone as much as she did Chloe. But she needn't have worried. Love was elastic. It stretched as far as it needed to and then a little bit more.

Abby had her mane of dark hair, unmistakably hers, with the same reddish highlights shining in the sun. She knew how difficult Abby would find it to get a comb through and how impossible it was to keep tidy. Her daughter. Her girls, she thought with a savage possessiveness. It didn't matter what her mother thought, or Dominic's in-laws either. They didn't know the situation so they weren't in a position to judge.

'Can we have an ice pop?' Abby asked.

Dominic answered almost automatically. 'Get one from the freezer but make sure you shut the door properly.'

Lucy felt a quiver of laughter inside. She must have said the same thing hundreds of times. Perhaps life here wasn't going to be as different as she feared.

She turned her head to see the more timid Chloe still hovering in the doorway. Lucy reached out her hand to encourage her inside.

'Did you find the climbing frame?' she asked softly.

'It's at the back of the garden,' Chloe said, nodding. 'There's a platform and a slide coming off it.'

'Wow!'

It was the reaction she'd been hoping for and Chloe nodded enthusiastically. 'And Abby's got a tree house, with a table in it and everything.'

'It's on posts,' Dominic explained as he listened to their conversation. 'The steps up to it are perfectly safe.'

Abby came back into the conservatory, clutching some paper and two ice pops. 'I got you a green one,' she said to Chloe, 'because that's my favourite.'

Chloe smiled her gratitude and took the ice pop. 'What's the paper for?'

'If you wrap it round at the bottom it catches the dribbles. That's what Jessie says. Come on, we're not allowed to eat them inside.'

Obediently, Chloe wrapped paper round the end and followed Abby outside.

'It's going to work, isn't it?' Dominic remarked, watching the pair walk between the trees and out of sight.

Lucy shifted uncomfortably on her chair once again. It was going to have to work. She could no more walk away from the opportunity to get to know Abby and share in her childhood than Dominic could walk away from Chloe. But…

'What are we going to tell the girls?'

His eyebrows raised slightly. 'About what?'

'Our marriage. It's hardly going to be a normal one. Even if we convince Jessie, the girls are going to know we aren't sharing a room and wonder why. At least I hope they will. We won't be doing them any favours if they grow up thinking that's normal.'

'Obviously when they're older we'll tell them the truth.'

He sounded faintly exasperated, but Lucy steeled herself to persevere. Whether he liked it or not the girls would talk. And if they talked people would gossip. And if they did that it would threaten to undermine everything they hoped their marriage would achieve. If their objective was to protect Chloe and Abby from other people's curiosity it seemed sensible to try and convince them their marriage was entirely normal in every sense. Which meant…

But she wanted him to suggest it first. She looked down at her hands. 'Do you want people…the girls…to think we're marrying for love?'

'I imagine they'll assume we are. That's why people usually get married.'

He was definitely irritated, but he hadn't really answered her question. 'So you're going to pretend you love me? Does that include when it's just us and the girls?'

He raked a hand through his sandy-coloured hair. 'I hadn't thought it through that far.'

'We're going to have to think about it a little. If we're engaged people are going to expect some show of affection.' She shrugged slightly. 'The girls will expect that too. I'd like to know what you're expecting of me, otherwise I'm going to feel awkward. We could get caught out a thousand ways if we're not careful.'

'I suppose so.'

She pushed home the advantage. 'For example, my mum would suspect something was wrong if she ever heard you call me Luce.'

'That's not likely.'

'You'd be surprised how many people do, and it's always bugged me. Michael used to call me Georgie.'

Dominic leant forward to lean his elbows on his knees. 'Why?'

'Because of my maiden name. Before I married I was Lucy George. There were two Lucys in my class and I got Georgie.'

'Your mother will hardly expect me to call you that.'

'No, but it makes a point. What are you called?'

He smiled. 'Dom.' He stood up and picked up the two mugs. 'Don't get too bothered by all this. We're not trying to pretend we've known each other for a long time. Let's keep to the truth as much as possible. We met just over a month ago and...'

'Yes?'

Dominic walked over to the dishwasher. 'And we started seeing each other.'

'A whirlwind romance?' she prompted. This was like getting blood from a stone. She didn't want to put words to it.

'I see what you mean,' he said at last. She fancied he straightened his shoulders slightly before he continued. 'We shall just have to try and act naturally round each other. It'll be fine. The odd kiss, perhaps. That's all.'

It was what she'd been aiming at, but her stomach flipped at the word kiss. Apart from a couple of fumbling kisses at school discos she hadn't kissed anyone but Michael. Hadn't wanted to. And yet the prospect of kissing Dominic wasn't unappealing. He had a nice mouth. Firm and sensual.

She swallowed, aware of the way her eyes had moved to look at his lips. Hurriedly she looked away.

'Actors do it all the time,' Dominic continued firmly. 'We'll just have to get on with it if the situation demands a show of affection.'

Lucy nodded as confidently as she could. It would be easier if there weren't too many people watching. She'd never been a performer. 'I suppose so.'

'The most important thing is for the girls to be protected. While they're so young they need to feel they're part of a normal family. They'll need that security when we tell them the truth. We'll just have to make sure everyone's convinced our marriage is just like everyone else's.' He looked across at her. 'It shouldn't be too difficult. The first kiss will be the most awkward. But in the end it will probably feel quite natural.'

He walked back into the conservatory. His eyes were looking at her thoughtfully and Lucy bowed her head slightly to hide from his scrutiny. She felt really shy. It was all this talk about kissing. It wasn't something that should be talked over. But it had to be done. No one must know their marriage was an empty sham or there was no point in doing it.

'Lucy?'

She looked up.

'Let's get the first one out of the way.'

She couldn't pretend to misunderstand what he was suggesting. To kiss now. With no onlookers. To get that first embarrassing kiss out of the way.

It made sense. In a hundred ways it made perfect sense. But to do it would mean she'd have to get out of the chair and walk across the space that separated them. And then what? Would he kiss her, or would she have to kiss him first? Was he expecting a touch of the lips or something deeper?

She swallowed nervously.

'What do you think?' he asked again, holding her eyes with his.

'Now?' Embarrassingly, her voice broke slightly in the middle of the word. She hadn't felt this nervous when she'd been kissed for the first time all those years ago. To be honest, she could barely remember it. Simon Wetherington from the year above, she seemed to think.

She stood up and forced her arms to relax at her sides. 'I suppose it's a good idea.'

In the end Dominic came most of the way towards her. Two steps only before she felt his hands warm on her arms.

'Ready?'

She nodded and closed her eyes.

Everything slowed down as she waited for his lips to touch hers. One hand left her arm and touched the hair hanging over her face, gently pushing it back. She could feel his breath. And then he kissed her.

A feather-light touch, his lips warm and seductive. No one had kissed her for such a long time. She was so used to the feel of Michael, of security and friendship. But this was Dominic.

It should have felt like a betrayal, but it was so gentle it felt like a beautiful caress. Her lips moved involuntarily under his and her hand moved up to rest on his chest.

She was kissing Dominic.

The crisp linen of his shirt rested under her fingers and the heat of his skin warmed her hand. He felt surprisingly solid. Muscular. His arm tightened around her and she felt herself pulled in closer while his lips became more insistent, more persuasive. Dimly she was aware of the door opening, but she felt too intoxicated to do anything about it. She was kissing Dominic Grayling and it felt good. Her lips parted involuntarily and a soft moan escaped her.

'Why are you kissing Chloe's mummy?' an inquisitive voice asked.

They fell apart.

It took a moment for her breathing to steady and her legs felt weak beneath her. She didn't dare look at Dominic to see what effect their kiss had had on him.

'Are you going to get married?' Abby said, perching on the arm of the chair. 'People always kiss a lot if they are going to get married.'

Dominic reached out for Lucy's hand and held it tightly for a moment before he spoke. 'What would you both think if we decided to get married?'

'Would we live here?' Chloe asked, sitting on the sofa, her feet not touching the floor. 'With Abby?'

'We could be sisters,' Abby cut in.

Lucy hesitated before going across and kneeling in front of both girls. 'We don't want to do anything that will make either of you unhappy. We're thinking of getting married, but we want you to have time to get to know each other. And for you to know me,' she said, looking specifically at Abby. 'We all need to be sure we want to be a family together.'

Chloe frowned and looked straight at Dominic. 'You can't be my daddy.'

Lucy's heart lurched for him.

'You already have a daddy,' Dominic said steadily, 'who I know loved you very much. Your mum has told me lots about him. I wouldn't ever be a replacement for him, but I could be here for you. Do the things he would have done if he hadn't got sick.'

It was quite some speech. She wasn't sure she could have made one like it in the same circumstances.

'What would I call you?' Chloe wanted to know.

Dominic didn't hesitate, looking directly into the clear blue eyes of his biological child. 'Dominic.'

'Dominic,' Chloe repeated, trying out the word.

Lucy smiled tentatively at Abby. 'And you can call me Lucy.'

Abby smiled back at her without any reserve. They were very different people, these girls, Lucy reflected.

'Can we be bridesmaids?' Abby asked, with one flick of her unruly dark hair.

'I won't get married if you won't be.'

Abby nudged Chloe in excitement before turning back to Lucy. 'I'm not wearing pink. I don't like it.'

'No pink. It's a promise,' Lucy said in a voice that shook with emotion.

The decision was made. They were going to become a family.

Dominic reached down to pull Lucy up from her kneeling position, the feel of his fingers on her skin sending sparks of awareness shooting up her arm. It wasn't supposed to be like this, she reminded herself. It was going to be a marriage of convenience. Nothing more—*ever*.

'If that's settled we'd better get Lucy and Chloe's things in from the car,' Dominic said practically.

Lucy looked down at her hand in his. Could she really do this? For better, for worse? For the rest of her life? A man who didn't love her?

And then she felt smaller fingers slip into her other hand. Abby's fingers.

Her heart banged inside her with painful energy. Anything was worth this moment.

CHAPTER FOUR

SHE was engaged. Lucy shut the venetian blinds in her bedroom with a decisive pull on the cord. They couldn't have committed themselves more completely if they'd taken out half-page advertisements in all the major newspapers.

There was no going back. The girls had been told—and were pleased. That should have made her delighted. All the way here she'd been hoping Abby would like her, that Abby would like Chloe, that she and Dominic would get on sufficiently well to…

But she hadn't meant to kiss him.

Lucy placed trembling fingers against her mouth. His lips had been so warm, so persuasive. It wasn't what she'd expected or wanted— and she'd lay money on it not being what he'd wanted either.

She pulled back the duvet and sat down on the edge of the wide double bed. This was supposed to be a relationship based on respect and friendship, not passion. She couldn't allow anything to complicate this. There was far too much at stake. If she reacted like that every time he kissed her they were going to be in trouble before they'd really begun. She'd ruin everything.

Lucy smacked the feather pillow and snuggled down under the duvet. She was probably over-reacting. She was tired. That was all it was. That first kiss was always going to be awkward, and now it was over. Dominic had said himself it would never be as difficult again. He was probably right. In time it would no doubt become an automatic part of their lives together when the situation demanded it.

If she could just rid herself of the image of curling her fingers in his hair and the pulse of his heart beneath the fabric of his shirt.

She brought herself up short once again. It wasn't surprising she was finding it difficult to be in such close proximity to a man—after Michael. It was going to take some adjusting to. That was all this was. She snuggled deeper under the covers, letting the warmth soothe her and the scent of lavender about her pillow lull her towards sleep. She was so tired…

It took a while to register where she was. One glance at the illuminated hands of her travel clock showed it was only a little after two in the morning. She hadn't woken like this in months. After Michael died she'd scarcely made it through a night, but she'd thought that had long since passed. It must be the stress of the moment, of the engagement.

She knew from bitter experience there was no point trying to go straight back to sleep. If she'd been at home she would have made herself a cup of tea, perhaps done some ironing to make use of the time, but there was no way she was going to wander around Dominic's house in the middle of the night. Apart from the embarrassment if she met him, she knew she hadn't understood how to deactivate the alarm system.

She leant across and switched on the side light before pulling back the covers. She pulled on the zip of her holdall and took out a book. Then she hesitated, sure she'd heard something. It was enough to make her go to the door and open it a fraction. A small, soft whimpering sound echoed along the landing.

Chloe.

She should have expected this. Chloe's nightmares had been part and parcel of their lives for years. They were almost night terrors, they were so vivid and intense. She would wake up sobbing for Michael, crying for him. Over the months they'd slowly changed. Sometimes she just missed and wanted her dad, sometimes she imagined she was falling from a high cliff and no one could catch her, sometimes she was as small as a mouse and cats were chasing her and she had nowhere to go. What they all had in common was a deep rooted sense of insecurity.

She could have kicked herself for not taking more care. During the remainder of the day she'd been watchful of her, but there'd been no indication Chloe was finding this difficult. She'd tucked Chloe into bed and waited while she fell asleep. Everything had seemed fine when she'd checked on her later, but now her subconscious obviously had other ideas.

She threw the book carelessly on the bed and rushed to Chloe. As she reached the door of her room she heard muffled voices inside.

Her hand paused on the handle.

'Better?' Dominic's voice was asking in the same deep, comforting voice she recognised from their telephone conversations. It was hypnotically rich.

'A little.'

'Drink your milk.' There was a pause. 'Do you want me to wake your mum?'

She let go of the handle, unsure of what to do. Dominic had heard Chloe and gone to her. *And she was fine with him.* It was the strangest feeling. For so long it had been just the two of them.

'Tell me about your dad,' he was saying. 'Your mum obviously loved him very much.'

Chloe sniffed and Lucy's heart ripped in two.

'I've got a photograph of him.'

'May I see it?' Dominic asked in the same calm, quiet way.

Still Lucy hesitated outside the door. This conversation was too personal to interrupt. There was the sound of feet padding across carpet and then a zip being pulled back. Her hand went involuntarily to her mouth. She hadn't even known Chloe had packed a photograph.

'This was when he married my mum. I don't remember him like that, but Mum says he was a good rugby player.'

'What do you remember?'

Lucy leant her head against the door frame and fought back the tears. She felt guilty she wasn't in there with her little girl, guilty she hadn't been able to stop her pain—but so thankful to Dominic. He was saying all the right things. Letting Chloe talk. About Michael. It had been a long time since they'd spoken about him.

'He slept a lot and I had to be quiet. Sometimes he was sick.'

'He was very ill.'

'Yes,' Chloe agreed in a small voice.

'What are the good things you remember?'

'Sometimes we used to sit on the sofa and he would tell me stories. He used to make them up. He didn't need a book.'

Dominic's laughter rumbled quietly. 'That's really special.'

'And we used to play Fish.'

'What's that?'

Slowly, almost fearing she would intrude, Lucy opened the door. 'I thought everyone knew how to play Fish,' she said, moving towards the bed and smoothing back the ice-blonde hair of her daughter.

Chloe hiccupped and turned into her. Perching on the side of the bed, Lucy gathered her close. 'Did you have another nightmare?'

Chloe nodded into her shoulder.

'Do you want to tell me about it?'

The little girl shook her head.

'She was calling for her dad,' Dominic said, standing up.

Lucy's eyes met his above the top of Chloe's head. 'I'm glad you heard her.'

'I should have put her in a room nearer to yours. I didn't think. I'm sorry. I just thought the girls would like to be close.'

Lucy shook her head. 'I should have told you she has nightmares.' With tender fingers she stroked back the long blonde hair. 'But she hasn't had them for such a long time.'

Chloe sat up. 'Dominic came. I'm not frightened any more.'

He was on the point of leaving, but he turned to smile at her. 'I'll always be there when you need me, Chloe.'

She looked up at him and smiled. There was such a look of trust about her small face that it made Lucy's breath catch in her throat.

'Tell me something, Chloe?' Dominic asked, moving slightly closer. 'Is this game of Fish something you think I ought to learn?'

Her blue eyes sparkled. 'We could teach you. You need to have cards.'

'Playing cards?' She nodded. 'Wait there. I'll go and get some.'

The door clicked shut behind him. Lucy sat herself more comfortably on the side of the bed, cradling Chloe against her shoulder. 'I'm sorry I didn't hear you,' she said, kissing the sweet-smelling hair. 'Were you crying long?'

'Dominic heard. I'm glad you are going to marry him. I like him.'

'Do you?'

Chloe sniffed and Lucy reached for a tissue from the box she'd placed by the bed earlier. Then she'd thought it would be for hayfever, not for night-time tears.

'Do you love him more than Dad?'

The question caught her unawares. She'd always prided herself on telling Chloe the truth, and yet now it was impossible. The obvious answer was no, but the word stuck in her throat. How *did* she feel about Dominic? He confused her. Or maybe it was the whole situation that confused her. It was so difficult to distinguish.

'When I married your dad,' she started carefully, 'I knew we'd be together for always. Nothing changed that, Clo. Daddy didn't leave us because he wanted to. He was sick and his body couldn't manage any more. But your dad was a really special man. He wouldn't want us to be unhappy for ever. He'd want us to go on from where he left us. Do you understand?'

Chloe flung her arms around Lucy's neck and hugged tightly.

The bedroom door clicked open and Dominic stood holding out a pack of cards. 'One pack, as requested.'

There was something intimate about being awake in the early hours of the morning. It felt so private. Lucy tugged at the neckline of her overlarge T-shirt, bringing the material back up to cover her shoulder. She must look a complete mess. Too late to wish she'd paused to grab a dressing gown and brush her hair.

'First we have to have seven cards,' Chloe was explaining, with total focus.

'Do you want to do that? Or would you like me to deal?'

'You do it.'

Lucy interrupted quickly, 'Well, wait a minute. I'm getting cold. Budge up, Clo, and I'll get under the duvet with you.' If nothing else she could stop displaying quite so much leg. Not that Dominic appeared to have noticed. It didn't seem fair he could be quite so unruffled by her. It was different for her. She couldn't help but notice the small trail of chest hair dipping behind the navy dressing gown, but he was totally focused on his conversation with her daughter. *His* daughter.

Chloe moved over to make space. 'You mustn't look at my cards.'

'Promise,' she returned, settling her back against the mahogany slats of the headboard behind. Desperately uncomfortable. No doubt it had been designed by the aesthetically challenged Joseph Finchingly. And yet this was how Dominic chose to live. She ought to remember that. She was only going to be a part of his life because of a tragic mistake. He wanted nothing from her but Chloe.

Dominic reached for the cards and begun to shuffle them with strong, dextrous fingers. He really did have the most amazing hands. Amazing hands and a sexy mouth. She looked away and bit down hard on her bottom lip. She didn't want to be thinking things like this about him. It was…well, it was inappropriate. It broke every rule.

'Seven cards each?'

'You're very good at that,' Chloe said admiringly as Dominic dealt swiftly.

'Years of being at boarding school.'

'You went away to school? To sleep?' Chloe asked, her blue eyes wide and glittering in the soft light of the bedroom lamp.

Lucy picked up her cards and settled back to listen. It wouldn't hurt to know something about the man she'd promised to marry.

'From eight to eighteen.'

'Did you like it?'

Dominic pulled a face. 'I didn't have much choice. My parents lived abroad for most of my childhood and moved around a lot. I was lonely sometimes, but there was always someone to play cards with.'

His answer obviously completely satisfied Chloe, but not Lucy. 'What did they do?' she asked, unable to stop herself.

He glanced across at her, his eyes resting on her flushed face. 'My father was in the Diplomatic Service. For the last sixteen years of his life he was an ambassador.'

Lucy pulled up the thin cotton of her market T-shirt once again, embarrassed by his scrutiny. This whole marriage idea was getting more ludicrous by the minute. His father had been an *ambassador*. Normal people didn't do that kind of a job, did they? Her father had been a carpenter. Highly skilled, in great demand, but not exactly in the same income bracket as an ambassador. Her mother had been a crossing patrol lady to help with the family finances while she built up her pottery business. She and Dominic came from completely different backgrounds. There was no way this was going to work. They didn't have a single experience or expectation in common.

Except the girls.

'You have to ask for what you want, and if I have one I'll give it to you,' Chloe was explaining earnestly.

'And if you haven't?'

'I tell you to "go fish". That's why it's called Fish.'

While his attention was firmly elsewhere Lucy took the opportunity to look at Dominic closely. He did have that public school aura about him. Sort of relaxed, but incredibly confident. His face was vaguely familiar, as though some hidden memory was tugging at the back of her brain. It was nonsense, of course. It wasn't likely they'd met before. Maybe it was Chloe she saw in him? Maybe that explained the connection she felt when she was with him?

'Do I have to have one in my hand already?' he asked, looking at Lucy for clarification.

She jumped slightly. 'Yes. You're trying to make up sets of four. ''Go fish'' means you pick up from the centre pack.'

He smiled. He looked so relaxed. How could he be like that? Didn't he remember he'd kissed her? If he did, the memory of it obviously wasn't bothering him at all.

'You get to start, since you dealt,' Lucy told him, almost crossly. He ought to feel as uncomfortable about all this as she did. It just wasn't fair.

'Okay,' he said, shifting his cards in his hand. 'Chloe, do you have any threes?'

'Go fish!' she said, almost jumping out of the bed in her excitement.

He picked up from the centre pile. Lucy looked at him. 'Do you have any threes, Dominic?' He handed one across. 'Any more?'

His lips twitched. 'A lady with a killer instinct,' he said, handing across his last and watching her place the set of four on the table. 'I see I'm going to have to watch you.'

With an ease and bravado she wasn't feeling at all, she stuck out her tongue.

'Mum and I always beat Grandma at cards,' Chloe said confidently.

As the game progressed Lucy didn't display any aptitude at all, but her daughter didn't seem to notice. Her eyes were sparkling, her nightmare completely forgotten, as she piled up set after set in front of her.

It was a child's game, and yet Lucy couldn't concentrate. She couldn't remember who'd asked for what and anything she found was complete luck. Dominic hardly looked at her—which was good. He sat perched on the end of the bed, his eyes on his cards.

This had to be a magical moment for him. The first real connection between him and Chloe. From now on she was going to have to share her daughter. It was what she'd wanted when she agreed to this farce of a marriage, and yet it irked her that he could manage it all with such ease. Every nerve in her body was taut with tension.

Chloe let out a long yawn. 'Are we going to play again?'

'I think it's getting too late,' he said, picking up the cards in front of him.

'I'm not tired.'

'But your mummy is. Look at her eyes.' It was true—she had started to drop off, and her back was hurting from the wooden slats. 'Besides, you've won pretty much everything. I only got three sets and your mum just two. Let's call it a night and play again another time.'

Chloe was obviously more tired than she'd let on, because she smiled and snuggled down on to her pillow. Lucy flicked her legs out of bed and stood up. The night air felt cold and she rubbed at her arms. 'I'll stay here until Chloe's asleep.'

Dominic nodded. 'You'd better have this, then,' he said, untying the cord on his dressing gown.

'It's all right.'

'You're cold,' he said, shrugging off the dark navy cotton robe.

Lucy took it. There wasn't much else she could do. 'Thank you,' she said, trying not to notice how broad and tanned his chest was. She hadn't expected him to be quite so muscular. She didn't want to notice, and yet in the intimate twilight it was impossible not to be affected by him.

'Right, if you ladies are all right I'll head back to bed.'

'Thank you,' she replied, hating the embarrassment she could hear in her voice. She sounded about fifteen. She didn't feel much older either.

'Goodnight, Dominic,' Chloe said sleepily from her pillow, her voice almost inaudible.

Lucy scarcely heard her. She stood clutching his dressing gown against her cold body. Dominic stayed motionless too, his pupils dilated and his eyes focused on her.

'Put it on, then,' he instructed, his voice unusually husky.

Lucy slipped her arms into the sleeves, trying to tell herself it was nothing, no more than the loan of a sweater, trying to keep her mind off the fact that it was still warm from his skin.

'Very fetching,' he remarked, making for the door. 'You look…very fiancée-like.'

And he was gone.

Just a glimpse of a tanned back before he shut the door. What was happening to her? Every nerve was raw. Every sense had been awoken into zinging life. She didn't want this. It was rather like pins and needles after you'd been sitting on your foot—when the numbness wore off it hurt.

She pulled the belt tight with trembling fingers, a strange vortex of emotions swirling inside her. This wasn't supposed to be happening.

She'd thought she'd been prepared for everything. And she had been—everything but this. But *him.*

She'd only ever had such intense feelings for Michael. And even they had grown over time. She'd never experienced this kind of instantaneous awareness or the nervousness that went with it. She was awash with a hideous uncertainty about what Dominic might be thinking of her. Had he noticed the effect he had on her? Was it totally one-sided? Did he regret telling the children they were to marry?

Lucy looked down at her daughter's pale eyelids, shut fast, with something approaching envy. She'd never felt less like sleep in her life.

'Coffee?'

Lucy linked her fingers casually behind her back and tried to look as if 'the morning after the night before' syndrome was something she was very comfortable with. Of course nothing had actually happened—but it felt as if it had. Something had shifted—for her, at least. Maybe it was just an awareness of a possibility. Just knowing she was capable of feeling attraction again made such a difference.

'Coffee would be lovely.' The rich, heady aroma of freshly ground coffee assailed her nose.

'There's some croissants on the side if you'd like them. They should still be warm.'

In an effort to hide her embarrassment she walked over to feel the temperature. 'I was expecting cereal.'

'Put it down to a great bakers' on the corner,' he replied. 'I got these yesterday, but it's even better if you can be bothered to walk down and get them fresh.'

'But they're crisp. That's quite unusual for England.'

Dominic brought across a steaming mug of coffee to where she had perched herself on a high stool. 'A croissant connoisseur? This coffee might be a bit strong.'

Lucy glanced down at the dark liquid. 'That's great. Thanks.' She picked up the croissant and absent-mindedly started to unravel it. 'I'm sorry I overslept. Where are the girls?'

He smiled. 'I'm surprised they didn't wake you. There're making a tent out of duvets.'

'Nothing unusual there, then.'

'We ought to do that.'

Lucy's hand paused, her eyes shooting up to his face.

'Take them camping,' he clarified.

She swallowed nervously. 'Chloe would love that. At least she will if you guarantee you won't let a bug within two hundred metres of her. She's a bit nervous of things like that.'

'Abby would love the bugs and think it heaven if it rained.'

Lucy laughed and dipped her croissant in the coffee. 'I've never been able to understand Chloe's nervousness. I love the outdoors.'

It wasn't a surprise to discover Lucy loved the outdoors. Dominic realised with a sudden awareness that it was how he'd begun to picture her. If he conjured an image of her it was always outside, vibrant and alive, with the sunlight bringing out all the autumn colours of her hair.

And Eloise? She belonged in an elegant room, surrounded by brilliant minds and razor-sharp conversation. It was where she'd been most comfortable, with the cool aloofness of her beauty drawing all eyes to her. It was what he'd loved about her. And now he was going to marry Lucy. There couldn't be two more dissimilar women.

Dominic watched the way she continued to untwine her croissant. It was strangely fascinating, the way her fingers moved over the flaky pastry. 'Where did you learn to eat a croissant like that? It's very French.'

'We travelled there. Michael and I. During our year out.'

Michael. The man she'd loved. Abby's biological father. A man he didn't know. Would never know.

She talked about him so often. Of course he'd died less than two years ago, whereas he'd had six to become accustomed to Eloise's death. He'd forgotten so much about her. Somewhere over the years she'd become just a memory. A fond one, but it didn't give the searing pain it had once. Guilt, yes, he still felt that. If only he'd managed to persuade her that a life without children would have been a good one. But she hadn't listened, and if she had there would have been no Abby. He hesitated. No Chloe. He'd got that wrong. If she hadn't insisted on having a baby there would have been no Chloe.

Blonde-haired with ice-blue eyes, a memorial for ever of the woman he'd loved once. As Lucy had loved Michael.

'How long did you travel for?'

'A year.' She dipped the croissant back in the coffee. 'We married so young, and we weren't ready to try for a family so we sold our first house and set off. We weren't that imaginative. We did South Africa, Australia, New Zealand, Thailand and France. Everyone said we were crazy, but I'm really glad we did it. I've got some great memories.'

'I bet.'

'Did you take a year out?'

Dominic shook his head. 'Never felt the need to. With my parents travelling so much I'd been to so many places. I wanted to put down some roots, make a home.'

'I suppose so.'

Did he detect disappointment in her voice? As though she'd recognised yet another thing they didn't have in common. And there were plenty of those. Apart from the children, there really wasn't anything.

It didn't matter. This was the woman he was about to tie himself to. In every quantifiable sense it was the perfect arrangement. Mutually beneficial. For the sake of the girls. There was nothing personal about it. So why did he hate the sound of disappointment in her voice?

Without thinking, he broke off a piece of croissant, irritated at the way his thoughts were leading him. Everything Lucy did was a sensual experience. She ate a croissant as though it were a sensory indulgence, savouring each mouthful and licking her fingers. It was unnecessary. It was messy. He didn't want his life messed up. He liked it just as he'd got it organised. He liked order and form. He liked the rhythm he'd built into his day. It was impossible to imagine Lucy wouldn't change that.

She sat back and licked a flake of pastry off her finger. 'So, what happens now?'

'Abby goes to ballet. I've booked her and Chloe on a week-long holiday course.'

Lucy's eyes widened slightly. What was it he could see in her face? Surprise, certainly. Irritation?

'Abby goes every Tuesday,' he continued, hating the way he felt the need to placate her. 'I didn't think Chloe would like to be left behind so soon after arriving.'

'You could have asked me.'

His irritation sharpened. Of course he could have asked her, just as he'd asked her about the hundred and one other things they'd had to organise over the last month. But ballet? Every little girl did ballet, didn't they? 'I thought she'd enjoy it.'

'Possibly. She's never tried. You can't just make assumptions about what Chloe will or won't like. Are they happy to take beginners?'

Now he felt worse. He'd no idea whether the place dealt with girls who'd never donned a tutu. 'It's a ballet school. I imagine it's what they do. I thought we could use the morning to find a ring.' He glanced down at her left hand relieved to see she'd already removed the narrow gold band she'd worn previously. 'We could get the wedding rings at the same time.'

'Possibly—but the fact remains you should have asked me before you organised anything for Chloe. If this marriage is going to work on any level we need to work as a team.'

'It's only ballet—'

'Chloe's not a very confident girl, and I'm not sure she'll want to go to yet another new place today. I know you're used to making your own decisions, but so am I. If we're going to go through with this then I need to have an equal say in all decisions that concern the girls.'

Dominic looked at her in exasperation. After all they'd discussed she couldn't be getting second thoughts now. They were too far into their arrangements. The small civil ceremony was arranged for the twentieth of August. 'I'm sorry if you think I've been high-handed. I genuinely thought she'd enjoy it, and we do need the time to get a ring. It'll be better if you have one to show off when I introduce you to Vanessa and Cyril.'

She frowned.

He felt strangely reluctant to carry on this conversation but he forced himself. 'Eloise's parents. I've invited them for dinner.'

It was going to be a difficult meeting. He watched the way her hand stilled as it reached for her mug. Did she know how astounded—outraged—his in-laws were going to be at his choice of new wife? Or was she merely annoyed he hadn't asked her first?

'When?'

'This evening.' Two spots of colour burnt on his cheekbones as he realised he'd been wrong again. He should have asked her. 'I should have run it by you first. I'm sorry. From now on I'll do that.'

'Thank you.'

'Do you want me to postpone it?'

'Now we've told the girls we're getting married I ought to meet Eloise's parents. It's probably better to do it quickly.' She looked up at him, her brown eyes troubled. 'What do I wear?'

Eloise would never have asked such a question. She'd always known. His eyes flicked over Lucy's white cotton dress, long and floating with a low, scooped neckline. It was gypsy-like. Beautiful. Sexy. He pulled his gaze back to her face. 'Something black?'

'Oh.' She put the mug back on the counter carefully. 'After we've bought the ring I think I ought to buy a dress.'

CHAPTER FIVE

LUCY hated to admit it, but Chloe was in her element at ballet school. She'd looked with envy at all the little girls dressed in baby-pink leotards and net skirts. Abby looked less happy. Maybe she'd been concerned about the wrong little girl when she'd made her objection.

Chloe's hair had been swept up into a tight little bun with complete ease, and it was obvious she'd be in heaven if she came home with one of those nauseating pink outfits. But Abby? She'd had to be coaxed into her outfit simply because it *was* pink, and her hair had positively refused to be scraped back into the regulation style.

'Does Abby like ballet?' she asked an unusually taciturn Dominic as they drove away.

'I imagine so. All her schoolfriends seem to go.'

And they probably did. All those little girls with high-achieving mothers who drove about London in their completely inappropriate four-wheel drive cars. Ballet for your daughter was

probably the new black for any upwardly mobile mother about town, she thought spitefully.

She glanced across at the fixed profile of the
man beside her. Probably not the moment to
question him too much. He'd been the one
who'd had to suffer the morning tantrum and
the daughter doing an impression of a clinging
limpet. Chloe's eyes had sparkled from the
minute she'd been told where she was going.

'Do you know where we're going to get this
ring?'

'I've a friend who's a jeweller.' He paused
while he shifted gear. 'A good friend. I rang
him last week and told him I was planning to
marry my girlfriend.'

'Was he shocked?'

'I expect he was, but he's a good enough
friend to keep his opinions to himself.'

Which rather put her in her place, she
thought. Lucy let him drive in silence as the
reality of what she was doing started to bite.
She was going to get engaged to a man she'd
known only a few weeks. From this day on
she'd be living a lie. The outside world would
see a couple, whereas the reality would be
something so very different. It made her feel
uncomfortable—and somehow desperately sad.

'Do we have to pretend this is the real thing? While we pick the ring?' she asked suddenly.

'It is,' he replied, reversing his car precisely into a nearby space. 'We're not pretending we're getting engaged; we're actually doing it. And in a month we'll be married.'

He swivelled out of the car and shut his door with unnecessary force. It was the first indication he wasn't finding this as easy as he'd have liked her to believe. She shouldn't have been surprised. It wasn't so very different for him. Dominic knew what it felt like to get engaged for real. Perhaps he'd even taken Eloise to this same jeweller friend. And now he was with her—not because he wanted to be, merely because of a tragic mix-up. He was going to buy a love symbol for a woman he didn't intend to love. That was really very sad—for them both.

She lifted her hand and swiped quickly at her eyes. The least she could do was keep herself together. The last thing Dominic needed was a snivelling woman at his side. They were doing this so they could be there for both girls. She needed to keep herself focused and just get on with it.

Dominic went to put money into the meter, coming back with a ticket seconds later. 'Will two hours be long enough?'

'I should think so. How difficult can choosing a ring be?'

'You wanted to get a dress too,' he reminded her, opening the car door to leave the ticket inside.

'I haven't had much call for anything very smart.' *And I don't want to*, she could have added. Her lack of suitable clothes only seemed to underline how unsuited she was to this new life. 'What else do I need to do for this evening? Am I cooking?'

He looked surprised. 'You can leave that to Jessie. I've already rung her.'

Of course he had! Lucy immediately felt foolish. Dominic's life was a well-oiled machine. It was foolish of her to imagine she'd have any real part in it.

'I'm sure she'll talk over the menu with you when she arrives,' he added, as though he sensed her unease.

'I wouldn't know what to suggest.'

'What kind of ring do you want?' he asked, with an abrupt change of subject.

'I don't know.'

'What kind of ring did you choose with Michael?'

It was hard enough to be doing this without being reminded of Michael. The whole thing seemed a sacrilegious parody of something beautiful. 'We didn't bother. We went straight for the wedding band.'

He stood straighter. 'Don't you like jewellery?'

'It was more of a financial decision than a style one,' she said as airily as she could manage. 'So this whole ring thing is a first for me. How much do you want to spend?'

'Just tell Jasper what you like.'

Lucy heard the edge in his voice. Was money something she wasn't supposed to mention? He probably thought it took the romance out of the situation. But then there wasn't any, was there?

She could choose any ring she liked. No budgetary consideration at all. She'd never imagined she'd be in this position. It was the stuff of fantasies. Or should be. What would it be like doing this for real? Okay, he'd said it was real, and in a way it was, but in every way that really mattered it wasn't. She felt so small, so frightened. She looked up at him, searching his eyes for the same reassurance she'd seen in them at the very beginning.

He didn't fail her. 'It'll be all right,' he said softly, taking her hand. His thumb moved softly against her skin. 'Our marriage is going to be based on honesty and friendship. That's more than many people have. Think of the ring as a symbol of our agreement to parent our girls together, to share in their future.'

The sensation his thumb was arousing made her feel quite giddy. It was such a small, insignificant touch, and yet it had her wanting so much more. He made her remember what it had been like to be held close against his hard body, feeling the warmth of his breath on her cheek. She wanted to belong. To experience passion.

Or at least the prospect of passion. Someone to love and be loved by. A future where she could know she made the world a better place for someone just by being there.

Instead she was being offered friendship and honesty. It sounded dry and dusty to her. Hadn't he felt the connection between them when he'd kissed her?

Obviously not. She'd tried to convince herself her reaction had been entirely in her imagination but she couldn't fool herself any longer.

But if Dominic felt nothing for her...

She took her hand away. She was just going to have to try and play by his rules and make completely certain he never suspected she'd like the possibility of more.

Dominic reached up to push a discreet white button, turning to look at her briefly. 'Ready?'

She nodded, but he probably didn't see because he was giving his name to the crackling voice speaking through what looked like a small brass grid. As if by magic the door opened.

'Dom.' A man in bright red jeans came to greet him out of the comparative darkness. 'Come on through. Jasper won't keep you a moment.' Dominic's hand in the small of her back encouraged her forward. 'And this must be Lucy. We've just been wild to meet you.'

It was difficult to see clearly against the dark red walls of the hallway, but Lucy found her hands swept up in a friendly grasp by a blond-haired man who was no taller than her five feet five inches. Dominic put his arm around Lucy and she found herself leaning into him for support. 'This is Lucy Grayford, my fiancée. Lucy, this is Jasper's partner, Alistair Wood.'

'Hello,' she said in a small voice she didn't recognise as her own. Around her she let all the pleasantries go on, responding where she had to on autopilot. There was an unreality to everything, but she knew it wasn't a dream. She could feel the warmth of Dominic's body next to hers, smell the soft sandalwood scent on his skin. The deep timbre of his voice seemed to vibrate through her and the feel of his hand resting lightly on her waist was distracting. Intimate. Certainly no dream.

'Dom! You're early.'

Jolted into life, Lucy spun round to look at a tall, athletic man with vibrant green eyes. His hair was still wet from the shower and his T-shirt was a little damp, presumably from the same cause.

'Some of us get up in the morning,' Dominic replied, grasping Jasper's hand. 'This is Lucy.'

Jasper immediately pulled her close and kissed both cheeks. 'I'm thrilled to meet you. I was beginning to despair of Dominic. He's a man who ought to be settled down.'

'Really?' she murmured, trying to keep the smile on her face steady.

'You've met Alistair, of course,' Jasper said with an airy wave behind him. 'He's going to put the kettle on while I create something of genius. Now, you two come with me into the inner sanctum. Let's get the business of the day done before we talk.'

He led the way through a couple of doors and finally into his workshop. Everywhere was neat and precise, except for the scattered pile of papers on an oak desk. Each sheet was covered with squiggles and swirls where he presumably had tried out ideas.

It was irresistible. She walked over to the desk and picked up a sheet with one sweeping design dominating the page. 'This is beautiful.'

'That one?' Jasper said, moving closer and reaching for the paper. 'I wasn't sure about the top part. I want it to give the impression of freedom, but of intense security. The way the metal, unbroken, sweeps round to hold the diamond—' He broke off and shrugged his shoulders. 'At the end of the day it will only be a necklace.'

'Perhaps not to the woman who wears it,' Lucy objected.

The green eyes flashed with approval. 'Quite true. I like to think there's a spiritual dimension to my work. You aren't at all as I imagined you'd be,' Jasper said, putting the paper back on the desk. 'Dom wouldn't describe you.'

'I said she was very beautiful,' Dominic protested, sitting on a high stool and moving Lucy round so she rested against his thigh. A natural, casual movement of two people who should be in love—and yet Lucy felt like a mannequin. His hand rested casually on her hipbone and she could feel the soft warmth of his breath on the back of her neck. Every sense was prompting her to relax and enjoy the physical sensations. It would be so easy to lean back against him, run her hand along the length of his denim-clad thigh, turn her face towards his, kiss him... It was too dangerous. For him it would be part of the pretence, but for her it was becoming something very different. And that wasn't what he wanted.

'She *is* very beautiful,' Jasper replied warmly. 'A beautiful brunette.'

Very unlike Eloise. He didn't say it—but Lucy could hear the words hanging in the silence.

'You're a fortunate man, Dom.'

'I know.'

He almost sounded as if he meant it. Lucy hated it. For the sake of the girls it was necessary to convince everyone they were in love, but it felt dishonest.

'What sort of ring do you have in mind, Lucy?'

'It doesn't matter.'

Dominic's hand moved to her neck, brushing away the soft tendrils of hair. 'You'll have to tempt her,' he said in a surprisingly throaty voice. She could feel her body tense as his fingers moved against the softness of her skin.

'Shouldn't it be Dominic's choice?' she asked, pulling away.

Jasper laughed. 'Well, Dominic?'

'Isn't a diamond the usual thing?'

'I think we'd better ignore him if that's his level of contribution,' he said, walking across to the locked cabinet behind him. He looked back at Lucy. 'I see you as more fire than ice. So, gold rather than platinum?'

'I prefer gold.'

Jasper nodded. 'Let's decide on a setting before we turn our attention to the stones. Try this one.'

He passed across a gold mount with angled clips from all sides. Self-consciously she slid it over her knuckle and held out her left hand for inspection. The white marking on her finger showed painfully behind the delicate setting of the ring. 'This is lovely,' she said quickly, desperately wanting this whole farce to be over. A barren ring for an empty marriage.

It didn't matter what she wore. An engagement ring should mean you were loved. That there was someone in the world who thought of you as their treasure. Even the most beautiful ring couldn't compete with that if it was given without love.

'Dominic?'

'If Lucy likes it,' he said doubtfully. 'It looks a bit of a mess to me.'

'It needs its eyes. Its soul,' Jasper said, echoing Lucy's own thoughts. 'If we keep the petals in diamonds, what do you think about a different stone for the heart of the ring? I've just bought the most perfect emerald. I'd like to use it in the centre. It's almost the exact shade of your scarf, Lucy.'

She hesitated, waiting for Dominic to say something. A 'perfect emerald' sounded expensive, and she didn't feel able to offer much of an opinion. This ring was stage dressing for his world, not hers.

'Dominic?' Jasper prompted. 'Her dark colouring is made for emeralds.'

Lucy turned to find Dominic's eyes were resting on her profile. A small muscle twitched in the side of his face and he swung away.

'Tea on the terrace.' Alistair's bright voice sounded at the doorway. 'And a surprise. We have an unexpected visitor.'

'Unless it's someone we like, tell them to go away.'

'Fionnula.'

'Ah,' Jasper said, as though resigned. 'Tea on the terrace it is, then. You've met Fionnula, I suppose?'

Lucy looked questioningly up at Dominic. He didn't fail her. 'Not yet.'

'Really?' His voice was full of incredulity and something she couldn't quite identify.

'Lucy and I haven't been together long. We've let the outside world look after itself while we concentrated on the girls.'

At least that part was true.

'Probably a wise decision. And the ring?' Jasper asked as he covered the setting with a plain cloth.

'Use the emerald.'

His friend nodded, as though it had been what he'd expected. 'Right. I'll get the ring over to you as soon as I'm through.'

Dominic nodded and made way for Jasper to pass in front of him. He took hold of Lucy's hand to prevent her from following. She looked up questioningly. 'I should have told you about Fionnula. She's Eloise's cousin.'

'Cousin?'

'And my assistant,' he added quietly as he moved towards the door.

Lucy's heart sank lower than her shoes. This was going to be like skipping through a mine-field.

'You were going to meet her tonight anyway. She's coming to dinner with Vanessa and Cyril. She's their—'

'Niece. I can piece that bit together.'

'And very close to them. Since Eloise's death she's been something of a surrogate daughter to them.'

Lucy watched him walk through the door and knew she had no choice but to follow. She arrived in Jasper's comfortable sitting room moments behind him, but already a stunning blonde was kissing Dominic's cheek and laughing up at him.

'Fin,' Dominic said, holding her away from him, 'I'd like you to meet Lucy.'

Fionnula had scarcely registered her standing in the doorway, but she was forced to do so now. She stepped back, keeping one beautiful hand lightly on Dominic's arm. 'Lucy?'

'Lucy Grayford. My girlfriend.'

'I see.'

Two short syllables conveyed a world to Lucy, but one glance at Dominic was enough to convince her he was unaware of the other woman's instinctive dislike. If she were honest, Lucy had to admit it was shared. She hated the way Fionnula posed, transferring her weight on to one hip so she presented a perfect silhouette. She hated her flat vowel sounds and envied her board-like flat stomach. But, most of all, she hated the proprietorial hand resting on Dominic's arm.

'Yes,' Lucy said, stepping further into the room to offer her hand. 'I gather we were going to meet tonight? At dinner?'

Fionnula smiled—almost. It didn't reach her eyes and Lucy was certain the other woman's glance was pure appraisal. She took her hand with an elegant flick of the wrist. 'So you're the single mother staying with Dominic? I confess we were curious.'

'Widowed,' Lucy corrected, feeling her back stiffen.

'Ah, yes. Widowed. You've a little girl about the same age as Abby, don't you?'

'Her name's Chloe.'

But Fionnula had already lost interest. She'd turned back to Dominic almost before she'd finished her question and was laughing up at him.

Lucy waited for Dominic to say something. It would have been nice if he'd walked across the room to be nearer to her. Maybe this was exactly the moment for one of those casual displays of affection they'd practised. But nothing. He stayed beside Fionnula.

Instead Jasper said casually, 'He kept Lucy very quiet, didn't he? But that's always been Dom's way when something matters to him,' and then, as Alistair brought in the tea, 'About time. Let's go out on to the terrace. Make the most of British summertime.'

Lucy followed them outside, feeling more lonely at this moment than she'd ever done before. The conversation moved freely between the group and no one seemed to notice Lucy had gone quiet. She was glad of that. It gave her an opportunity to look more closely at Fionnula.

She was exquisitely beautiful in a cultured, high-bred way. She had the face of a china doll—large blue eyes, impossibly perfect skin, high cheekbones and blonde hair. The blonde hair was similar to Chloe's. Slightly darker and expensively highlighted, but, age for age, it would have been identical. It was like a cloud of sunshine on top of a perfect package. She wore it framing her face, flicking outwards in a playful swish. It was hard to believe Dominic could remain immune to such beauty if she wanted him. And the more she watched the other woman the more certain she was that she did.

Lucy sipped her tea. Had Eloise resembled her very closely? Cousins didn't always, but sometimes... If Eloise had been so perfect it was obvious why Dominic was so certain he'd never love again. How could any woman live up to a predecessor like that? Not even Eloise's cousin, it seemed.

'We need to be going, Lucy.' Dominic cut in suddenly on her thoughts.

She jumped, putting down her cup and saucer on the bamboo table.

'You haven't finished your tea,' Alistair protested.

'It doesn't matter.'

'We've got the girls to collect from ballet,' Dominic explained.

'It's Chloe's first time. I don't want to be late.'

'Of course not,' Jasper agreed, standing up and catching both Lucy's hands in a friendly grasp. 'And there'll be plenty of other times for us to meet up.'

'Dominic,' Fionnula said, reaching for her bag, 'do you think I could have a quick word in private before you leave? Business,' she said, turning her head briefly to look at Lucy.

'Tonight—'

'If you confirm a couple of dates with me now I can ring them later this morning.'

Dominic shrugged, but moved into the hall-way. Lucy could hear their voices becoming fainter.

'You know, Lucy, if Dom had been inter-ested in Fionnula it would have happened by now,' Jasper said softly, following the direction of her gaze. 'She looks like Eloise, of course, but they're completely different. Eloise was a darling. Fionnula can be fun, but she not Dom's kind of woman. I didn't know she was coming. I'm sorry.'

He'd meant to be consoling, but the confirmation that Dominic's first wife had looked like an angel—and been one too—was scarcely comforting. 'Does she love him? I'm sorry. I shouldn't have...' she murmured, freeing her hands.

'If she loves anything but herself it'll be his reputation. She's a very ambitious lady.'

'Ready?' Dominic popped his head round the door.

'As ever,' she returned, forcing a bright smile to her lips, not entirely understanding what Jasper had meant. 'Let's not be late.'

Outside, she immediately turned towards the car.

'Where are you going?'

'To get the girls.'

'We've got to get you something to wear tonight. Vanessa and Cyril won't be as accepting as Fionnula.'

Lucy's heart missed a beat. If the blonde ice maiden had been 'accepting' she was about to be thrown to the wolves when she met Eloise's parents. 'I thought we couldn't be late?'

'We've plenty of time. Ballet doesn't finish until twelve.'

She crossed the road after him. 'So you lied?'

'I rescued you.'

'From?'

He stopped abruptly. 'I'm not an idiot. I know how difficult you found that. But it'll get easier. Fionnula will be on the phone to Vanessa and Cyril by now, and they'll have an idea what to expect.'

'Meaning?'

He shrugged. 'Meaning…not to expect a carbon copy of Eloise.'

Lucy looked down at her sandals, taking surprising comfort from her cerise-painted toenails.

'Lucy…' Dominic took her gently by the arms and held her steadily until she looked up. 'You don't have to be like Eloise. I don't want you to be. I just want you to be there for the girls. Our girls. You can be yourself.' She blinked painfully. 'All right?' he asked, looking into her eyes.

'I suppose so. She didn't seem to like me very much.'

'Fionnula? That's just her way, and I did rather spring you on her. I suppose I should have told her more about you,' he said, letting her go.

'Why didn't you?'

'Don't know, really. We were still making our arrangements. It always seemed as if there was going to be another time.'

That was hardly a satisfactory answer. Lucy sniffed and searched fruitlessly for a tissue. 'I think she likes you.'

'I certainly hope so. She's my assistant. A friend.'

His words were blithely unconcerned. Jasper had been right, then, when he'd said Dom wasn't interested. It was curious. Few men could have resisted such a beautiful woman, but perhaps she was only a pale copy of Eloise.

'Fin was fantastic after Eloise died. She's been very supportive—acted as my hostess more times than I can remember.'

'Right.'

He looked at her sharply. 'I know Cyril and Vanessa had started to hope something might develop between us, but nothing ever will. We're friends.'

'I see.' There didn't seem much point in saying anything else. Dominic obviously couldn't see what was blatantly apparent to everyone else. Or maybe he just didn't want to see that Fionnula had aspirations to be more than a friend. The woman was like a piranha.

Dominic crossed the road and waited for Lucy to catch up. It was good to be away from Jasper's scrutiny. He hadn't rescued Lucy so much as himself. Hell, this was more difficult than he'd imagined.

'Did you like the ring?'

Lucy nodded. Small, soft tendrils of hair bobbed around her face, and her brown eyes were still troubled. 'Is it going to be too expensive? It sounded like Jasper was getting a bit carried away.'

'With the emerald?'

Lucy nodded again.

'You're going to be wearing the ring for a lot of years. Better to have something you like. Besides, I think an emerald will suit you.' And he meant it. He hadn't realised until Jasper had said it how much the strong green suited her. But now he'd noticed it was difficult to stop imagining how Lucy would look if she bought a dress in emerald-green rather than the black Eloise had favoured.

He looked at his watch, frustrated by his thoughts. 'We've got forty-five minutes before we need to be back at the car.'

Lucy was Abby's biological mother and the woman who'd brought Chloe into the world.

That was all. He'd no business noticing anything about her. Not the way her hair curled, or the length of her neck, not the way she curved in all the right places, filling out that simple white dress as though it had been moulded on her. Certainly not the way she'd looked in his oversized dressing gown.

'If we're late I'll get a hefty fine.'

'I'll try not to take too long,' Lucy replied, and immediately he felt guilty. The whole situation was difficult but he mustn't take it out on her. She'd given up a lot to come to London. He had to remember that.

CHAPTER SIX

OVERALL Lucy felt she'd managed the afternoon well.

Abby had been a delight, her small face invariably grubby, her eyes darting with energy. But it had been her smile that had twisted Lucy's heart—a haunting echo of Michael's. She could see him in her mind's eye, sitting on some rocks, the wind in his hair, with exactly that expression on his face.

Already she couldn't imagine a future without Abby in it. She loved her as passionately as if she'd given birth to her. As passionately as she loved Chloe. They'd sat together over burgers, salad and fat crispy chips. Almost a family. Even the swim had gone well. She'd pleaded tiredness and sat out on the side, watching. The girls were happy. It should have been enough to make her happy too.

But always there'd been Dominic. She didn't believe in love at first sight. It was nonsense, and yet it was so difficult to explain what was happening to her. It was as though Dominic was moving through the world in sharper focus than everyone else was. Brighter somehow. She loved the way he was with the girls. Envied the way Chloe could rest her small hand on his water-glistened body and speak softly to him.

'Lucy?'

The brush in her hand stilled at the sound of his voice outside the door. 'Yes?'

'Have you got a minute?'

She put the brush down on the dressing table, feeling as though she might have conjured him up just thinking about him, and cleared her throat nervously. 'Have your in-laws arrived?' She moved across to pull open the door.

At the sight of him in his dinner jacket her throat contracted and she found it difficult to breathe. She'd been nervous before, but now she was terrified. He looked so different...so gorgeous.

'Not yet. I wanted to...wanted to speak to you before they arrive.'

'Is there a problem?' she asked, moistening her lips nervously. *Had he changed his mind? Had he decided he couldn't go through with their marriage?*

Lucy's hands spread nervously over the soft fabric of her dress. It hung in graceful folds around her curves. She'd never owned anything so sophisticated—or so lovely. The miracle underwear the shop assistant had insisted on had done seriously fantastic things to her cleavage. Her ample bosom filled the low neckline in a way that made her wonder whether it was a little too much.

'No problem.' His eyes flicked across the simple black dress she'd chosen. 'You look incredible.'

'Thank you.'

Dominic could see the pulse at the base of her neck beating, the dark shadow of her cleavage. He could picture a necklace nestling in the shadows. Something like Jasper made—with a diamond catching the light. He cleared his throat. 'Jasper sent over your ring.'

'Oh.'

He pulled out a small black box from his jacket pocket and held it out to her. 'I assumed you'd rather put it on privately.'

Lucy took the box with fingers that shook a little. This was the moment of no return. Choosing the ring had been difficult, but this was the final acceptance of their need to spend their future together. 'I would much rather do this privately,' she agreed quietly. 'Have you looked at it? Is it beautiful?'

'Open the box.'

She lifted the lid, carefully holding the container straight. Inside was a dream. A sparkling flower God would surely have designed if he'd thought about it. *Her ring.* Made for her. So beautiful.

The symbol of a future without love. 'It's lovely.'

'Put it on.' He reached forward and took the ring out of its velvet cushion.

With a slight hesitation Lucy held out her left hand. Slowly he slid the narrow band over her knuckle and pushed it in place. Lucy blinked away the tears that blurred her vision. This felt so real. So permanent. 'It's lovely. Thank you.'

Dominic didn't let go of her hand. Instead he pulled her closer. She became mesmerised by the unexpected warmth in his blue eyes. This moment meant something to him as well. It had to. It might not be love. It might not be passion. But there was gentleness there. She could see it in his face.

And without a word, he kissed her. Softly. His mouth gently touched hers—and then he released her. 'It's going to be fine.'

'Yes.'

She wanted to believe that.

The ring was heavy on her finger. Despite being so used to wearing one, it felt strange. *Dominic's* ring. She felt cold suddenly. If this were for real there would have been more laughter. He would have put his arms around her and held her. She would have felt safe. Loved. It was possible she would never be loved again in her entire life.

'Are you ready?' She nodded, struggling to appear calm. 'Would you like a drink before they arrive?'

If there'd ever been a moment where Dutch courage was permissible this had to be it. 'I think so,' she said slowly.

With slow deliberation he interlaced his fingers in her trembling cold ones. 'Come on, then.'

Dominic led her down the hallway. The stairs were wide and they walked side by side. Was this how people had felt on the way to the guillotine? Even as the thought popped into her head she dismissed it. She was being ridiculous. It wasn't so bad. She'd agreed to marry a man for the sake of their daughters—a nice man, a good man.

'How long before your in-laws arrive?'

'Ten minutes or so. They're usually prompt.'

'Is Fionnula travelling with them?'

Dominic let go of her hand and ushered her towards the kitchen. 'I imagine so. Are you ready to announce our engagement to Jessie? We may as well ease ourselves in gradually.'

Lucy nodded. She wasn't ready, but she couldn't imagine ever feeling as though she was.

'Jessie?'

The friendly brunette she'd met earlier turned, wiping her hands on a cloth. 'I must say you both scrub up very well.'

'Don't we?' Dominic returned, the lines on his face crinkling attractively. 'We've got some news for you.'

'If you're going to tell me they've cancelled you can jolly well go and ring round some other friends. My Salmon Coulibiac is not to be wasted.'

'Would I dare?'

'Actually, yes,' she returned with a swift smile at Lucy. 'My talents have gone entirely unappreciated for years. I only stay for Abby.'

Dominic's eyes glinted with appreciation. Lucy watched with curiosity, despite her nervousness. She hadn't known what to expect of Jessie. She didn't move in a world where anyone paid people to do anything much. Perhaps a childminder, or a cleaner once a week, but not someone who would come in and run your daughter's life and home. But Jessie was more than an employee; she felt like family. She'd welcomed Lucy as though she'd always belonged there, and she'd set about the preparations for the dinner party after a very one-sided discussion about what she should cook. In just a few short hours she'd become a firm favourite with Chloe, who, following Abby's lead, was stealing home-cooked biscuits from the tin without any qualms.

'Lucy and I have got engaged.'

'Oh!' Jessie let go on a breath, dropping the tea-towel. 'I was hoping… I mean, that's just wonderful. Really, really wonderful. Have you chosen a ring?'

Shyly, Lucy held out her left hand.

Jessie grabbed it and looked in awe. 'It's stunning. I'm so, so pleased for you both. I think it's just marvellous. Do the girls know?'

Lucy nodded.

'We told them yesterday,' Dominic cut in. 'If everything's ready in here, come and have a drink with us.'

'I'll have a sherry,' Jessie said, picking up the tea-towel. 'Oh, I feel quite light-headed. I'm so excited. I'll just give the sauce a quick stir and be through in a moment.'

Dominic smiled, his blue eyes glinting with every appearance of enjoyment. 'Lucy?'

'I'd like some wine.'

'Dry white?'

'Lovely.' She watched him walk from the room before turning to look at Jessie. 'I hope you don't mind. I know it's been a bit quick...'

'Of course not. Why should I mind?'

'I don't know, really. I suppose because it's all so sudden. We've only just met...'

Jessie closed the oven door. 'I think it's absolutely fantastic,' she said firmly. 'It's long since time he put the past behind him. He loved Eloise. Of course he did. But she's been gone a long time now and he needs to move on. He's been on his own far too long.' She smiled suddenly. 'Of course there're going to be many broken hearts.'

Lucy's mind immediately flew to Fionnula. It didn't seem right to ask Jessie too many questions, but she couldn't resist a simple, 'Really?'

'"The Thinking Woman's Crumpet,"' Jessie said, her round face breaking into an even wider grin.

'I'm sorry.'

'Haven't you seen that one? I just loved it. Couldn't resist putting it on the inside of the cupboard door, just to annoy him.' She walked across the kitchen and opened one of the top cupboards. 'Next to the coffee. I thought I'd better keep it near a mild stimulant.'

Lucy walked across to look at the magazine page tacked to the door. Unbelievably, it was Dominic's face that peered down on her.

'Women can't seem to resist that craggy charm of his. Or maybe it's the boyish enthusiasm. You get him on the Romans in Britain and he can bore for England. But you must know that,' Jessie added self-consciously. 'When the results of that poll came out he hated every moment of it.'

Lucy stood mesmerised. *Dominic was a historian.* He'd never lied to her. Everything he'd said about his job began to fall into place. 'I see myself as an educator.'

But a television presenter? She hadn't dreamed of such a thing. Now she understood why his face was so familiar. It wasn't because of Chloe. Or at least not entirely. She must have seen his face a thousand times. Picked up one of his books in the bookshop. Yet she'd not made the connection.

'Are either of you coming through?'

'Just coming,' Jessie said, hurrying through to the lounge.

Lucy slowly shut the cupboard door as Dominic appeared back in the kitchen.

'Looking at Jessie's idea of humour?' he asked, walking towards her.

'Something like that.' She looked up at him. 'I didn't know.'

'I'm glad.'

She frowned. It seemed a strange thing for him to say.

'It's just a job. History's my passion and I've a knack for making other people interested. That's all it is. I don't like all that kind of nonsense.' He took hold of her shoulders and twisted her round to face him. 'It's one of the reasons why I don't want anyone to know anything about the IVF mix-up. For the sake of the girls it has to be kept private. No one must know why we've decided to get married. Let's do this for the girls.'

Lucy nodded. Everything made sense. Even Fionnula. Jasper had told her the other woman loved his reputation. She understood now. From the little she knew of her she could see how Fionnula would love the status marriage to Dominic Grayling would bring.

Instead it was her, Lucy, marrying the thinking woman's fantasy. And it was just a façade to protect the girls from press intrusion. It had to be done. It made complete sense. But it didn't feel that simple.

As she looked up into his handsome face it wasn't simple at all. She wasn't so very different from the women who'd voted in that poll. The understated sex appeal that had brought him a television career was very attractive. She could feel the pull of it every time she looked at him. She wanted to believe there could be more. She wanted to feel his lips on hers again. Know what it was like to be held in his arms because he really wanted her to be there.

'Lucy?' His eyes had followed her thoughts and his blue eyes had darkened to the colour of a midnight sky.

She pulled away. He mustn't know how she was feeling. It would complicate everything. He'd think she was impressed with his fame and money. Their marriage was for the girls. It was so she could know Abby and give Chloe a father. All of that was more important. *It was, wasn't it?* She took a step backwards.

'I understand now. No one must know.' As she reached the door she turned back. 'I feel stupid. I should have recognised you. I knew you were familiar. I thought it was just Chloe.'

Dominic thrust his hands into his pockets. 'It probably was.'

'Maybe. I feel really foolish. I'm not right for you. No one's going to believe it.'

'Let me be the judge of that.'

Lucy laughed nervously. 'I'll do it. I'll marry you because of Abby and Chloe. But a dress doesn't change the girl. I'm not a dinner party sort of person. I don't know how to do all this.'

Dominic crossed the space between them. 'Nothing's changed, Lucy. Be yourself. No one will expect anything else.'

'Your in-laws?'

'Will find it difficult because you're not Eloise. It's not personal.'

Lucy so wanted to ask, *And Fionnula?* But she didn't dare. The beautiful blonde obviously wanted more, but if Dominic was unaware of it there was nothing she could do about it. He suddenly seemed an aloof stranger. Someone she hadn't expected to meet in a million years.

She walked through the door, determined to play the part expected of her. Jessie was there to meet her completely unaware she'd just dropped a bombshell.

'Is this your glass?'

Lucy accepted the fine-stemmed glass and waited while Jessie handed a second to Dominic. 'To you both,' Jessie said, raising her sherry glass. 'I hope you'll be incredibly happy together.'

Lucy sipped obediently. The chances of that seemed even more remote than they had half an hour ago. She wasn't cut out for this kind of life. She was a quiet, country kind of girl. She didn't want to live in a goldfish bowl, with every second woman wanting to be in her position. She liked to shut the door and know she was home.

'To the future,' Dominic said, resting his arm around Lucy's shoulders.

The doorbell rang and Lucy jumped as much from the contact of his arm as from the shrill sound.

'Do they know yet?' Jessie asked with gleeful anticipation.

'Not yet.'

'Positions, men. I'll get the door.'

With a flurry of activity she left, her half-drunk sherry abandoned on the side.

'She didn't seem to mind. In fact, she seemed genuinely pleased,' Lucy remarked, playing with a coaster on the side table. 'I'm dreading this.'

Dominic placed his glass down on the side and crossed the room. 'Lucy, trust me. It's going to be fine.'

'They'll never believe—'

'What?'

'That you want to marry me.'

'Why?' His hand flicked at the unruly lock of hair falling from her tight chignon. 'Because you're not intelligent?' Her breath caught in her throat. 'Beautiful?' With slow deliberation the back of his hand moved along her jawline. 'Any man would be lucky to have you as his wife, Lucy. I know this is too soon. I know you don't want—' He broke off. His hand curved about the base of her neck and pulled her closer. Lucy closed her eyes and let it happen. She needed him.

And, God help him, he needed her.

Dominic tried to pull back but he couldn't. He hadn't meant to kiss her, either now or earlier. There was no one watching. No one to impress. And yet he could only give way to impulse. There was something irresistible about the trembling fullness of her mouth. He wanted to reassure her, keep her safe. He'd always wanted that. From the first day, he realised with a shock. There was something so vulnerable about her—and yet so strong.

Slowly, deliberately, his mouth met hers. His hand curved into the softness of her hair. Even now, pulled back into a tight chignon, it couldn't achieve sophistication. She was raw. Vibrant. *Like Abby.*

This was all for the girls. She was forcing herself to agree to a loveless marriage. Just a business arrangement. He had to remember that. Pulling back, he looked into her dark brown eyes. 'Abby needs you.'

'I know.'

'And Chloe needs me.'

'Yes,' Lucy said on a whisper. 'I do understand. I'll try not to let you down.'

'Excuse me, darlings,' Fionnula announced as she emerged into the room.

Lucy took an urgent step back. Her smile faltered as she took in the elegant blonde. In evening dress, she was a vision in peacock-blue. Swathes of chiffon passed over the gym-perfected body and her legs looked endless. Behind her was an older couple, the woman unmistakably related to her. The same high cheekbones and impossibly flawless skin.

'You must be Lucy Grayford.' Vanessa Carpenter stepped forward, her beautifully manicured hand stretched out. 'How do you do?'

Lucy found she responded automatically. 'Hello.'

'Has Jessie taken your coats?' Dominic asked, coming to her rescue, kissing his mother-in-law lightly on one cheek. 'What can I tempt you to drink?'

Lucy could feel Vanessa's curious, slightly antagonistic appraisal and wondered what Fionnula had said about her. She pushed her ring hand firmly behind her back. She didn't feel ready for that kind of conflict. If she could have slipped the ring off her finger she would have been tempted to do so. This was going to be a difficult evening for Eloise's mother.

'I'll have a bourbon, as usual,' Vanessa answered. 'Is Abigail unwell, Dominic? I understand from Cerise you've cancelled Abigail's piano lesson tomorrow.'

'With Lucy and Chloe so newly arrived it seemed sensible,' Dominic returned, handing her a glass.

'But discipline and consistency is so important. You mustn't let anything get in the way of her education. Eloise wouldn't have wanted that.'

Dominic moved closer to Lucy. His hand reached for hers and gave it a conspiratorial squeeze. She could almost hear him say, Might as well be now. 'I'm so glad you could join us this evening. I particularly wanted you to meet Lucy.'

They looked at her, and in Vanessa's eyes Lucy thought she could see fear.

'She's agreed to become my wife.'

The silence was deafening.

Fionnula's smile slipped slightly. 'You're engaged?'

'Guilty,' Lucy said, holding up her ring hand.

The difference between this reaction and Jessie's was marked. There was no outpouring of joy, no good wishes for the future.

'How very sudden.' Fionnula smiled archly up at Dominic.

'Very sudden indeed,' Vanessa concurred, her smile brittle. 'We had no idea. No idea at all—did we, Cyril?'

Her husband ignored her.

Fionnula flicked those long legs and sat on the edge of a cream sofa. 'We didn't have much chance to talk earlier, Lucy. I was so taken up with a project Dom and I are working on together. What is it you do, exactly? He hasn't said.'

'I'm a teacher.'

'Fascinating,' Fionnula said insincerely.

'Bloody poor money, I always think.' Cyril turned his attention away from a painting. 'It's not something I'd have wanted Eloise to do.'

'No,' his wife agreed quickly. 'But then Eloise was so gifted...'

Dominic laid a protective arm on Lucy's shoulder. It was good to know he was there, but strangely he needn't have worried. She didn't expect Eloise's parents to be pleased he was remarrying. With every fibre of their being they must wish their daughter were still alive.

'No one teaches for the money,' Lucy said softly. 'I love seeing children produce work they didn't know they were capable of—'

'Eloise was a lawyer,' Fionnula cut in. 'She had the most brilliant mind.'

Lucy turned to look at her. 'I know. Dominic's told me a lot about her.'

Vanessa sat gracefully on the chair opposite, crossing her legs at the ankles. She was in her mid-fifties, maybe early sixties, Lucy surmised. Poised and elegant, with the kind of bone structure that meant she'd be beautiful into her eighties. *Chloe's biological grandma.*

'Fionnula tells me you have a daughter yourself?'

'Yes.' She had the same blue eyes as Chloe. 'Is she bright?'

'Extremely,' Dominic interrupted. 'Shall we go through to the dining room? Jessie won't forgive me if it spoils.'

He led the way through to the spacious dining room and settled the women into their seats.

'As a teacher, Lucy, I'm sure you understand the importance of discipline. I'm really very concerned about Abigail's musical tuition being interrupted. Eloise was a very gifted pianist herself. I feel I owe it to her to make sure her daughter has the same opportunity.'

'I don't think,' Dominic interrupted as Jessie came in the room with the first course of tomato and feta soufflés, 'that Abby particularly enjoys the piano.'

Lucy felt miserable. All she could think of was how she would feel if she were in Vanessa's shoes. This woman had lost her daughter, and was obviously frightened she would lose her grandchild too. Her whole manner of speaking was brittle and nervous.

'I'm thinking of letting Abby take a break,' Dominic continued. 'Perhaps she'll be more suited to another instrument when she's older. Lucy and I will have to talk about it.'

Fionnula looked sharply across at her. When she spoke her voice was sugar-coated. 'Does *your* daughter play anything, Lucy?'

'I'm afraid not.'

'Aren't you musical?'

Lucy met her blue eyes calmly. 'Not particularly. But I think Chloe may well be, and I'll encourage her. I don't believe any child should be forced to do something they're not particularly suited for. If the piano isn't Abby's forte then something else will be.'

Fionnula flicked her blonde hair. 'I love music. Do you remember that delightful concert we went to at the Albert Hall, Dom? I still remember the flautist. What was her name, now?'

'Lucienne Chaillet,' Cyril announced ponderously. 'We saw her again this spring, when we were in Paris.'

'I can't imagine any daughter of yours not being musical, Dom,' Fionnula said with a soft touch on his arm. 'Both you and Eloise shared such a love of it.'

'But not at six,' Dominic said firmly. 'Fionnula said you've just got back from Hamburg, Cyril. How did you find it?'

Lucy relaxed as Dominic steered the conversation in a different direction, but it was only going to be a short respite. His late wife's family were not about to give up their influence easily. And who could blame them? If they loved Abby they must be very frightened that a new stepmother coming in would ruin their relationship with her.

It was all the more poignant because Abigail wasn't their granddaughter. It was *Chloe* who was Eloise's biological child. *Chloe* who bore the family resemblance.

The evening passed interminably slowly. Jessie's Salmon Coulibiac was delicious, but Lucy found it difficult to taste anything. The conversation swirled about her, and all the while she was aware of Fionnula's veiled hostility and Vanessa's pain. There was nothing she could do to help her. It was with immense relief she saw Jessie bring in cheese and biscuits.

'I don't think I can eat another thing,' Vanessa said. 'Shall we take our coffee through to the sitting room? I should very much like to know some more about Lucy, particularly since she's going to be so involved in my Abigail's life.'

'Jessie?' Dominic called. 'We'll have coffee in the sitting room.'

'Are you intending on teaching in London?' Vanessa asked, sitting on a chair by the reading light.

Lucy sat opposite her. 'Not immediately. I intend to concentrate on getting to know Abby.'

Vanessa nodded sadly. 'On Thursdays Abigail always comes to me. We spend some time on her French. My mother was French, you know. Both Eloise and Fionnula were bi-lingual by the time they were seven.'

'It's possible that may have to change,' Dominic said, taking the seat next to Lucy. 'We'll have to blend the two girls' interests.'

Lucy could feel Cyril's resentment skim across the room and interjected quickly. 'Of course we won't do anything which would damage your relationship with Abby. I'm sure she loves spending time with you. I know Chloe likes nothing more than being with my mum.'

'We'd hoped Fionnula might one day—' She broke off but it was palpably clear she'd hoped her niece might one day take her daughter's place. It was in the way she looked across at her and sighed, as though all her dreams had come crashing down.

Fionnula looked down at her knees in mock embarrassment, but Lucy wasn't fooled. Where Vanessa made her feel sad, Fionnula made her angry.

'I've just realised what's missing from this room,' Cyril announced. 'Eloise's photograph.' He turned accusingly on Dominic. 'From the mantelpiece.'

All eyes turned on Dominic. For once he looked ruffled. 'I put it away. I thought...'

'Whatever will Abigail think if her mother's picture is put away the minute you take up with another woman?' Cyril challenged. 'She's still the girl's mother, Dominic.'

'I don't think she's even noticed.'

Lucy intervened softly. 'I don't need you to do that, Dominic. I appreciate the thought, but I'd prefer you and Abby to have your memories around you.'

She could feel her heart fill up with emotion. He'd put away the picture of the woman he loved *for her*. It touched something deep inside her. But she didn't need him to do that. 'Please put her photograph back.'

Dominic looked at her questioningly and she nodded emphatically. Quietly he stood up and walked over to the long sideboard, hesitating slightly before opening the drawer. Without glancing down at the photograph he took it out and crossed back to the mantelpiece.

The room was silent as they looked at the picture.

Eloise had been beautiful. So very, very beautiful. Lucy looked at the soft features of the angel she'd feared. The photograph was in black and white, but it didn't disguise the glory of her incredible hair.

In some ways she was like Fionnula, but Eloise's features were more perfect, her eyes soft and dewy, full of love. 'Did you take the photograph?' she asked Dominic, already knowing the answer.

'How did you know that?'

'Her expression. You can see the love in her face. It's a beautiful picture, Dominic. You must keep it out.' She stood up and smoothed down her dress. Dimly she was aware of Vanessa; her gently lined face looked suddenly older and very, very sad. 'I do hope I'm not being rude, but I'm incredibly tired. I'll leave you to chat with your relatives and take myself to bed.'

'Lucy—'

'No, really.' She smiled around at the assembled company, forcing back the tears that were burning at the back of her eyes. 'It's been a long day and I've a bit of a headache. It's lovely to have met you. Goodnight.'

It *had* been a long day, but that didn't really explain how she was feeling. Everything was so confusing. She didn't want to think about it now—not when she was so tired.

Thankfully, Dominic let her go. She couldn't have borne it much longer.

Once upstairs, and safely in the sanctuary of her room, Lucy walked over to the bedroom window and looked out on the street lights. *So different from home.*

All around her there were millions of people, all busy going about their normal, happy lives. If any one of them knew she was going to marry Dominic Grayling they'd assume she was a fortunate woman. Instead…

She walked slowly over to the wide double bed and sat down on the edge. Could she really spend the rest of her life like this? Alone? Living a lie? She twisted the engagement ring on her finger and slid it off, placing it on the bedside table. And as the feeling of loneliness and isolation closed in on her she wrapped her arms tightly about her body and cried. The hot tears burnt her cheeks as she let herself curl up into a ball of pain.

Eventually there was nothing left to cry. She lay quiet and exhausted.

'Lucy?' Dominic tapped lightly on the bedroom door. 'Lucy?'

Quickly she wiped her face and went to pull the door ajar. 'Have they left?'

'Just.'

Lucy searched his face for some kind of strain and found it. It was in his eyes and in the two small lines that furrowed his forehead. He must have found the evening difficult. More difficult than she had, which was saying something.

Dominic would have haunting memories of Cyril and Vanessa in the immediate aftermath of Eloise's death. He'd remember how they'd been part of Abby's life, from the sadness surrounding her birth to now. He must know how his remarriage would hurt them. He would see the pain in Vanessa's eyes, just as she'd done.

She turned back and sat wearily on the edge of the bed. 'How were they? After I'd gone?'

Dominic shrugged off his jacket and threw it across the chair just inside the door. 'They're still grieving for Eloise,' he said as he loosened his tie.

'Of…of course.'

'It's not personal.'

'No.'

Dominic moved to sit beside her. 'And… how are you?'

'Me? I'm fine.'

He looked into her face. 'You've been crying,' he said softly.

She wanted to deny it, but knew her face would be blotchy, her eyes red. 'I didn't like that. Any of it.' She pulled at an invisible thread on the skirt of her dress. 'Are…are you sure we shouldn't tell them? About why we're doing it?'

'I'm sure.' He laid one warm hand across hers, stilling her nervously twitching fingers. 'Lucy, it was never going to be easy. We're getting married for the girls. It's all about them. Not Cyril and Vanessa. Not your mother. Not even about us.'

Lucy looked at his eyes, drinking in their strength.

His mouth twisted. 'If there was even the slightest whisper I was involved in an IVF mixup our lives wouldn't be worth living.' His thumb moved against her palm. 'It's one of the more unpleasant side effects of working in television. All the hospital's efforts to keep the girls' identities secret will have been for nothing. It *has* to be a secret.'

'But they're hurting…'

'And so are we.' He linked his fingers with hers. 'But the girls *aren't*. We have to do it,

Lucy. Until they're old enough to be told the truth. We have to keep the whole business between ourselves.'

His hand was warm in hers. Strong. They sat in silence and Lucy listened to the nothingness. How many years would she have to lie to Michael's mother? To her own? To Vanessa and Cyril? But, deep down, she knew they had to do it—for Chloe and Abby.

'Agreed?' he said at last.

Lucy nodded without enthusiasm. He leant across and kissed the top of her head. She closed her eyes and let her head rest on his shoulder, taking comfort from the steady beat of his heart.

So much pain—but there was no choice.

CHAPTER SEVEN

'WHAT'S happened here?' Dominic asked as he strolled into the kitchen, his shocked eyes taking in the chaos of the room. 'It looks like World War Three just broke out.'

'We made muffins,' Abby said excitedly. 'Lucy showed us.'

There was lumpy batter spread liberally over the high-gloss worktops and a considerable amount of flour on the floor, much of which had been trodden through the conservatory. He'd never seen his kitchen look like this. Jessie managed to create the most amazing confections without a hint of this kind of disaster.

'I'm sorry about the mess,' Lucy said, reaching for more kitchen towel. 'We were just about to clean it up.'

'Good grief,' he said, turning about, 'all this for a few muffins.'

'I'll get it sorted,' she said hurriedly. 'They've spilled a bit of flour, that's all.'

Which was something of an understatement, Dominic thought, as he took in her white-splattered black trousers and the smudge of flour on her cheek. 'Do you always make this kind of mess when you cook?'

Lucy stopped scooping flour and looked at him. 'I suppose so. I—'

'Do you want to do the kitchen or the girls?'

She looked down at her clothes and brushed at the flour on her trousers. As the white smears spread she grimaced. 'I suppose I'd better do the girls and see to myself at the same time. I'm sorry—'

'Try not to shake too much flour off on the stairs, Abby,' he interrupted as his daughter began to dance about, 'or poor Jessie will have heart failure.'

'She won't, you know, Lucy,' Abby's voice said confidently as they left the kitchen. 'She says Daddy could do with a bit of messing up.'

Which was probably true, Dominic thought as he started to clear the debris. By rights he should hate this—the ordered regularity of his home changing. It was what he'd clung to for the past six years, since Eloise died. And yet Fionnula's gently worded criticism of Lucy's mess one day had found him defending the discarded pair of sandals on the stairs and the handbag left in the hallway. Lucy was too busy living to take much notice of how things looked and was simply not interested in whether the cushions were neatly placed.

She was like a fresh spring breeze blowing through his home. He'd heard the girls laughing from his study and he'd had to force himself to stay there. He'd made himself sit at his computer screen until he'd written a thousand words when he wanted nothing more than to join them. To join Lucy.

He leant back on the worktop and closed his eyes briefly in frustration. It wasn't supposed to be like this. When he'd proposed to Lucy it had all seemed so simple. They would go on living separate lives, both investing time in their girls. What could be more sensible?

He'd expected to make compromises, expected a period of adjustment. What he hadn't expected was the overwhelming desire to thread his fingers through her hair and pull her close. She'd stood in his kitchen, her hair looking as though it were about to fall down from the cheap plastic clip she'd put in it, her face and clothes plastered with flour, and he'd still thought she was beautiful. More than beautiful. He'd wanted to brush the flour from her cheeks and cradle her face between his hands. He wanted to see passion light up her velvet-brown eyes.

He stacked up the bowls and put away the paper cases. Maybe this inexplicable attraction wasn't so unexpected. Her husky voice at the end of the line during their telephone conversations had been compelling. The voice, the woman—she was so alive. If he'd thought about it logically he would have known this was a possibility. His physical reaction to her was the same as it would be to any beautiful woman in the same circumstances. It meant nothing. The woman he had loved, *did love*, he corrected urgently, was Eloise.

Dominic struggled to bring the image of his late wife into the forefront of his mind. It angered him that she was becoming less vivid. Sometimes now he would go for days when he didn't think about Eloise at all. He'd promised himself he'd never let that happen. He'd never allow another woman to take her place in his life. Eloise had *died* giving birth to his child.

He shook his head, as though it would reorganise his thoughts. *That wasn't right.* She'd died giving birth to *Abby*. But she'd still died because of him. He owed it to her never to allow himself to forget her. Anything else was a betrayal.

'We're clean,' Lucy said, coming back into the room. 'Or at least I am.' She ran her hands over the light Indian cotton sundress she'd changed into. 'I'm sorry about all the mess. I thought we'd be able to get everything straight before you came down.'

Dominic swept a pile of flour into his hand and dropped it in the bin.

'Abby said she'd never made muffins.'

Dominic began to stack the dishwasher, turning his back to her so he didn't have to see the way a dark strand of hair curled on her collarbone. 'Well, she certainly has now. Perhaps they're a little too young.'

'Do you think so?'

He glanced across. It was a mistake to look at her. He knew it the minute he allowed his gaze to move away from the dirty bowls. For a strong woman she was so absurdly vulnerable. She stood looking at him, her hair still perilously near to falling down and her wide smile faltering slightly. He knew he had to keep her at a distance but he didn't want her to feel bad.

'Probably not. They certainly enjoyed it,' he said, relenting.

Her face cleared instantly and her eyes sparkled. 'They did, didn't they?'

It would be so easy to move to hold her, to kiss her. Dominic struggled to swallow as he pushed down such an unworthy impulse. It wouldn't be fair—to Eloise's memory or to Lucy.

They had an agreement and he had to stick to it. Lucy deserved more than a casual physical relationship but he had no more to give. Certainly no heart. He turned to place the final bowl in the dishwasher. Besides, it was quite possible she wouldn't be interested anyway. As Fionnula had said, Lucy was very uncomfortable around him, and obviously struggling to adapt to a very different lifestyle than the one she was used to.

He shut the door and set the dial. Maybe marriage was unwise. And yet what was the alternative?

Lucy moved forward slightly, then stepped back. 'You've got a bit of flour…'

'What?' He turned.

'Flour. It's there.' She stretched out her hand, changing her mind at the last moment. 'On the back of your jeans. You must have leant on the worktop.' She let out that beguiling gurgle of laughter that sent his libido into orbit. 'I am sorry. Really. I don't usually cause such chaos.'

Dominic brushed off the flour, hating the way he was feeling.

'Are the muffins cooked, Lucy?' Abby asked, running back into the kitchen with Chloe close behind.

Lucy glanced across at the cooker timer. 'Any second now,' she said. 'Do you have any cooling trays?'

'Bottom drawer, left-hand side, Chloe,' Dominic said, pointing. 'These muffins had better be good.'

'They're brilliant,' Chloe said confidently. 'We used to make them all the time at home. They've got cheese in them.'

'That explains what was in the blue bowl then.'

The buzzer rang out shrilly.

'Or around the blue bowl, if I'm truthful,' he continued, fascinated by the way Lucy's dress floated out as she went to open the oven door. She was just so different. He'd never met anyone like her. Every movement she made was sensual. Perhaps in time he would cease to notice the shape of her legs through the thin cotton fabric? Eventually he would become used to her...

'That was Abby,' Chloe said, putting the cooling trays out on the worktop. 'She grated the cheese and most of it missed the bowl.'

'Only because Lucy wouldn't let me use Jessie's special grater. She said it was too sharp.'

Dominic met Lucy's eyes as she carried the muffins over, her tongue firmly gripped between her teeth. 'A wise decision.'

'I thought so. Stand back, everyone. These are hot.'

Abby could hardly contain her excitement. 'They're cooked! Can we eat them now?'

'Give Lucy a chance to get them out of the trays,' Dominic said, laying a restraining hand on her curly brown head. 'By the time we've got plates out, and made a cup of tea for me, they'll be ready.'

'Have you had a good day?' Lucy asked as she began to transfer the muffins across to the cooling rack. 'Fionnula implied you had a lot to do.'

He filled the kettle and turned to look at her. Was Fionnula right in thinking Lucy was lonely? 'We did well. I'm sorry I've got so much work on at the moment.'

'I didn't mean—'

'It's bad timing. I'd hoped to be so much further on by now. I didn't intend you just to be childcare.'

Lucy lifted the final muffin out of the tray. 'I always intended spending the summer with Chloe. It's lovely to have time with the girls.'

'Are they ready now?' Abby asked, leaning against the worktop, her nose practically resting on the muffins.

'If you had one now it would burn your mouth.' Lucy moved the plate away and glanced across at Dominic. 'I wasn't complaining. I really did just want to know what you're working on.'

'Did you know my daddy's on television?'

'Yes, I did.'

'And he's writing a book.'

'So I gather.' Her voice was dry.

Dominic curled his fingers into the soft curls of Abby's head and smiled across at Lucy.

'This series is about castles.' His smile broadened. 'I try not to talk about it all the time but it's a bit of a strain. Whenever I get working on something I'm a bit obsessive.'

Lucy reached out for the plates. 'How long do you have to finish this project?'

This was better. He could speak about work. He could concentrate on something other than the soft scent of vanilla soap that hung about her. 'We're on the final stages now. Fionnula's taken some amazing photographs for the book. That's what we were doing today—matching them up with the text. We've also finalised the locations we're going to film in.'

'When does that happen?' she asked, passing him a muffin.

'Late October.'

'Not that long, then.'

Lucy sat back and watched him bite into his cake, aware of the girls' faces as they watched for his reaction. It was crazy the way she wanted him to be impressed. Her heart did a tiny flip as he looked across the top of the muffin and winked at her.

This was a family moment. It was the reason why she'd agreed to marry him.

'These are fantastic!' Dominic pulled Chloe and Abby close to him. 'You two are geniuses. Does Jessie know she's got competition?'

Abby laughed delightedly, almost bouncing up and down in glee. 'I'm going to make muffins every day.'

Dominic's eyes flicked over to Lucy again, inviting her to laugh with him. 'Every day?'

'Sometimes we put apple in them,' Chloe said, standing a little on the edge. 'Or raisins, but I don't like them.'

'I'd like to try the apple,' he said, reaching out an arm to draw her closer.

Chloe's fair head curved into him and she hugged him tightly. Watching them, Lucy found it difficult to swallow. If Jessie saw them now she'd see an ideal blended family, but this was just the façade of something perfect. And it wasn't enough. With sudden clarity she knew it wasn't enough.

Not for her.

Dominic was handsome, clever and sexy. He was what hundreds of woman fantasised about—and he was committed to marrying her. He really, really loved their girls. But he didn't love her. And he didn't intend to. So moments like this were as good as it would ever get. She would always be on the outside, looking in. And it wasn't enough.

Somewhere along the line, almost without her noticing it, the all-encompassing grief she'd felt when Michael died had softened. She'd loved him, would always love him, but she had to go on. For herself as well as the girls. She'd thought there would never be anyone for her but Michael, but the healing her mum had talked about had happened and she was ready to love again.

Inside her head a voice was screaming in panic. She couldn't go through with it. She couldn't marry Dominic. She couldn't condemn herself to a life like that. How could she survive years of living with a man like Dominic Grayling and know he didn't want her to be there for herself alone? He didn't want to know what her favourite films were, or the name of her pet rabbit when she was six, or how she'd felt when she climbed the Eiffel Tower. He wasn't fascinated by her—as she was by him.

She was making tea in his high-tech kitchen and suddenly knew her life would never be the same again. Lucy turned round to look at him. *She loved him.* The way she felt around him wasn't just a physical response to an attractive man. It was something she'd seen at the very beginning when she'd looked into his eyes. It was kindness. An empathy for others. It was something indefinably Dominic. And she loved him.

'Aren't you going to have one, Lucy?'

Lucy brought her head round to look at Abby. 'As soon as I've poured the tea.'

Her hand shook slightly as she filled the mugs. This hadn't been the plan. But could she walk away from Abby now? Could she deny the chance for Chloe to grow up knowing and loving the man whose genes she carried?

Lucy carried across the tea, her face a mask.

'I meant to tell you I won't be in this evening.' Dominic took his mug.

'Oh?'

'There's an award dinner I've agreed to go to.'

Lucy's fingers played with the muffin case, slowly pulling the fluted sides away from the cake.

'It shouldn't finish too late.' His hand stroked Chloe's smooth head. 'We're not nominated this year but we won a couple of years ago. It seems churlish not to go. I knew you wouldn't want to go, so Fionnula's happy to come with me. She's very good at this type of thing.'

Lucy deliberately looked away. 'Do you want another muffin, Abby?'

'If there's anywhere you want to go...' He trailed off. 'Anyway, I'll take care of the girls tomorrow evening. Give you time to paint.'

Lucy nodded. 'They'll enjoy that.'

'We won't be making muffins, though!' he said, reaching for his tea and standing up. 'I better go and have a shower. I'll take my tea upstairs.'

It was stupid to feel so betrayed, and yet she did. Fionnula was his work colleague, but it didn't stop it hurting. Lucy gathered up the paper cases and screwed them into a tight ball. If Eloise had been alive she was sure he'd have taken her to the award dinner rather than her cousin. But he'd decided not to take Lucy and that hurt. Desperately.

A night's sleep didn't do much to improve her spirits. Knowing she loved Dominic made everything feel different—and it had been hard enough before. The award dinner didn't matter; what mattered was that he didn't see her as suitable. That he thought perhaps she'd let him down playing the part of the woman he loved.

The suspicion he was right made it acutely painful.

Lucy dried her hands on the kitchen towel. She had to be more positive. Life really hadn't changed that much. She was doing all the same things in a different place, that was all. It was what she'd expected when she'd agreed to marry Dominic.

In fact it was better than she'd expected. Now she didn't have to worry about money, and she really felt as if she had two daughters, not one. She should feel happy enough.

But...

It wasn't home. She still walked about the house terrified she might have moved something out of place, despite being told to treat it as her own. How could she feel anything else when she knew Eloise had agreed on the position of every cushion, every ornament? It was impossible.

'Jessie!' Lucy called into the garden, where the other woman was harvesting mint. 'Do you mind if I go into the studio? I want to stretch some paper before this evening.'

'Go ahead. I'll listen out for the girls,' Jessie said, coming in with a handful of strong-smelling leaves. 'Has Dominic had breakfast?'

Lucy took in the frown on Jessie's face and answered placatingly. 'He was late last night.'

'He's in the study. I'm beginning to think he lives there.'

'He's very busy. I'm sure he'll eat when he's hungry.'

'It's the third day running. What's the matter with the man?' She put the mint down on the chopping board and picked up a large cook's knife. 'He's going to end up pale and pasty, locked away in there all the time. What will his army of female admirers think then? I think you should put your foot down, I really do.'

'Perhaps he'll have a break when Fionnula arrives,' Lucy suggested, and was rewarded with a sharp look from Jessie.

'I'd watch that one,' she said, chopping the herb with unnecessary vigour.

Lucy just smiled and turned towards her studio. Fionnula wasn't a threat to her. The woman who stood between her and Dominic becoming closer was Eloise—everlastingly young and eternally beautiful. No living, breathing woman was ever going to be able to take her place. Though Fionnula didn't help, with her constant presence in the house, her resemblance to Eloise and her determination to make mischief.

She had to find a way of accepting that her life with Dominic was going to be exactly as he'd predicted when he'd proposed. He would carry on with his life and she with hers—but they'd share the girls.

Lucy shut the door and inhaled deeply. The room smelt of turpentine and paint. A few touches from home and it would be perfect. Over the last couple of weeks it had become a real sanctuary. Taking Dominic at his word, she'd spent his money creating a place she felt comfortable in. After the initial guilt had passed she'd even begun to enjoy choosing the furniture. There had to be somewhere in this monument to Eloise she was allowed to be herself.

Lucy kicked off her sandals and padded barefoot across to the wide table by the window. Already its wooden top was smeared with a rainbow of paint. Sable brushes stood in old jam pots. It was almost like her kitchen table at home.

Lucy reached up to get down a drawing board and lovingly smoothed out some watercolour paper before trimming it off. There was no reason for her to feel so dissatisfied. Everything would be fine—just not perfect.

And how many people actually managed to live the dream anyway?

'Lucy?'

She jumped at the sound of Dominic's voice. He so rarely came into this room. Her stomach flew up to her ribcage at the sight of him. This was the first time she'd seen him since she'd realised she loved him. It shouldn't have made any difference, but...

'Is there any reason why I shouldn't be away the first week of September?'

If things were different she could have smoothed the two lines in the centre of his forehead and kissed away the tiredness in his eyes. 'Not that I can think of,' she said, turning back to her roll of gummed paper tape.

'Do you think anyone will think it strange? It won't be long after the wedding.'

'They all know you're in the middle of a project.' Lucy shrugged and concentrated on cutting two long lengths and two shorter. 'I can't see a problem.'

She expected him to leave then. Previously he'd only hovered about in the doorway and escaped as soon as he possibly could. Today he hesitated. 'Chloe will be starting a new school.'

'Yes.'

'Do you think I ought to be there?' He crossed and sat on the flame-red sofa, moving a blue cushion to one side. 'I could rearrange if necessary.'

Lucy spun round on her chair to look at him. He looked completely out of place. At least…he *should* have looked out of place. But the more Lucy thought about it, the more she realised that, amidst all her clutter, he looked relaxed. Certainly more comfortable than she felt around his things.

It was hard to see him sitting there, his sandy hair ruffled where he'd been pulling his hands through it. He always did that. He would start the day immaculately groomed and reappear at the end of it like a mole emerging from his hole, wide-eyed and tousled. It must be hard going for him to look so exhausted so early in the day.

'I'll be there to see Chloe into school.'

'I know, but—'

'I don't think she'll have a problem,' she said, dipping a small sponge in cold water. 'She wants to be anywhere Abby is. The two of them are practically joined at the hip.'

'Perhaps we could do something the week-end after? To celebrate.'

'That would be nice.'

There was a pause before Dominic leapt up and walked closer to some bright paintings tacked on the wall. 'You've made a really good job of this room. Did Abby really do this?'

She looked where he was pointing, and then at Abby's name written in black pencil at the bottom of a picture. 'Of course. Look at the one on the left.' She gestured towards a picture of four people, each with a wide smiling face. 'It's us. You and Chloe have the yellow hair and Abby and I have brown. She said she was painting her family.' She spun the chair back and continued passing the sponge across the paper. 'It makes it all worthwhile, doesn't it?'

'Yes, it does.' His voice sounded unusual, strained. He moved to stand behind her. 'What are you doing?'

Even looking in the other direction, she knew he was there. Close. It made her feel self-conscious. Nervous, even. 'Damping the paper,' she answered calmly.

'Why?'

'It stops it cockling. If the paper wrinkles it's difficult to control washes and…just spoils the picture.'

She could feel his breath on the back of her neck as he bent forward to look at what she was doing. It made her remember how it felt to be kissed by him. He hadn't done that since the night he'd given her the ring and that seemed a long time ago now. If anything they seemed to be more awkward with each other than they had been at the very beginning.

But she hadn't loved him then. Hadn't believed it was possible she could ever love anyone after Michael.

'Do you have to do this every time?'

'It depends on the weight of the paper.' *If only he would just go away.*

She could almost feel what it had been like to be held against his warm body. Her imagination was firing in all directions and he didn't want her to feel this way about him. He'd be horrified if he realised how much she wanted him to kiss her again. 'If the paper's heavy enough you don't really need to, but there's no point buying great quality paper just now. I'm still only playing with ideas.'

'Lucy?'

She turned. Her face was only inches from his.

'Are you happy here?'

'Y…yes. Yes, I am.' He was looking at her intently. 'The girls are fine, aren't they?'

'I was meaning you. Are you happy? There's still time to call everything off. If you want to…'

Lucy felt ice travel from her head down to her feet. Had he guessed the way she was feeling about him? Was that why he was asking the question? 'D-do you?'

'No. I just wanted to be sure you were still happy with it all. We don't seem to have had much time to talk recently.'

'Well, you've been busy.'

'Yes.'

She was finding it increasingly difficult to breathe. This wasn't about the girls—it was about her. If he said he'd changed his mind then she would only see him when he collected or returned Chloe, only speak to him when they organised the changeover.

'I'm fine with it. Really.' She hurried on, not wanting him to speak. 'Nothing's changed, has it? I couldn't cope with losing Abby now, and Dr Shorrock said the other day it's still going to go through the courts.'

His eyes dropped to her lips. 'If you're sure.' He reached out and tucked one long corkscrew of hair behind her ear.

Lucy inhaled sharply. *He was going to kiss her. Again.* And she really, really wanted him to. Everything slowed down; her heartbeat became a solemn thud. 'I am. Very sure,' she said slowly.

If she just moved a fraction their lips would meet. It was there in his eyes. He wanted to kiss her as much as she did him. There was no one here to convince. It wasn't part of the agreement. This shouldn't be happening but she so wanted it to. With every thud of her heart she was saying, *please*.

'Dominic?' a female voice called from the distance.

Lucy pulled back, trying to tell herself it was just as well. If she'd kissed him she might have given herself away and then he'd have *known*. Whatever she did he would look at her and know she loved him, and he'd feel sorry for her because he couldn't love her back.

'Dominic, are you there?'

'Someone's calling you,' she managed. She was like some lovesick teenager. Her disappointment was almost like a physical pain.

She'd been so sure he was going to kiss her. Her lips were burning simply from the possibility of it.

'So this is where you are,' Fionnula said, stepping down into the studio. 'Am I early? We did say we'd meet at eleven o'clock, didn't we, Dom?'

Dominic swung round. 'Is it that time already?'

'Past, darling,' Fionnula said, with an intimate smile and a flick of her elegant hand at an invisible mark on his shirt.

'Right.' Dominic pulled his hand through his hair. 'I'll get back upstairs.' Without looking backwards, he left.

Lucy waited for Fionnula to follow. Instead, she spun round a full three hundred and sixty degrees, showing off every aspect of her perfect figure. 'So this is your studio?'

'Yes.' Lucy sat down and moistened a length of tape with the sponge.

'It's very bright.'

'I like it that way.'

Fionnula's acrylic-tipped fingers began to leaf through a file of Lucy's work in a way that made her itch to slap them away.

'Actually, this one is quite good.'

Lucy spun round to look at her properly. Fionnula was as impeccably groomed as ever. Her white suit didn't have a crease in it and her high heels clicked on the floor.

'Thank you.'

'Is this of Abigail?' Fionnula reached out and took hold of a small pen and ink drawing.

'Yes.'

'I like the way you've caught her profile, although I think her nose isn't quite so pointed.'

Inside, Lucy was burning with indignation. It felt like a violation to have this woman look at her private drawings.

'And this one is of Dom?'

Deliberately turning away, Lucy concentrated on taping the paper to the board and smoothing it straight.

She heard the sound of shuffling paper as Fionnula moved through the pile. 'There's quite a few of him.'

'He's got an interesting face to draw.'

'Dom photographs beautifully too. I must show you some of the shots I've taken of him. Eloise always had a favourite one by their bed.'

'Really?' Lucy resisted the temptation to turn around. The other woman was meaning mischief. She could hear it in her voice—that sugary sweetness that could only mean trouble.

'I was saying last night how very difficult you must be finding it—living in Eloise's house.'

Lucy stuck down the final length of tape. Reluctantly she turned round. 'It's Dominic's house too.'

'But it's such an expression of Eloise. She poured everything into this house and its design. Sometimes I've thought it isn't quite healthy the way Dom won't let anything be changed. It's almost a shrine.' Fionnula smiled insincerely, her teeth so white they must have been capped. 'Of course she was a quite remarkable woman. Did Dom tell you she got a first from Oxford?'

'Yes, he did.'

'She was quite brilliant, of course. Aunt Vanessa was so worried when she suddenly announced she wanted to get married at twenty-one.'

Lucy stood up and perched on the edge of her desk. 'Really?'

'She met Dom at university, you know. The fear was that Eloise wouldn't reach her full potential if she married so young. She'd an amazing legal mind. Razor-sharp. But in the end it didn't matter. Dom would never have stopped Eloise doing anything. He adored her, as I'm sure you know.'

Lucy let the table-edge push into her palms. Fionnula might be a stunningly beautiful woman on the outside but she was nothing but a cat within.

'I suppose we should have expected he would ultimately remarry someone completely different.' She shook her blonde hair confidently. 'He wouldn't want to be reminded.'

'Life moves on,' Lucy said calmly. She wouldn't give her the satisfaction of knowing how deeply her comments were hurting.

'And so does time. I can't stay chatting any longer,' Fionnula said dulcetly, with a glance at her delicate wrist-watch. 'Would you ask Jessie to bring us up a couple of coffees? I think Dom and I are going to be ensconced up there for two or three hours at least.'

'I'll tell her.'

'Oh.' She stopped and spun round on her heels. 'I meant to warn you. Dom and I were photographed as we left the award dinner. Did he mention it? I'm sure it won't cause any comment because we're so often together...' She let her words hang in the air before she shrugged elegantly. 'Since Eloise died I've been her deputy at so many of these events.'

'He says you enjoy them.'

Fionnula's insincere laugh echoed around the studio. 'Not exactly that, but he knows he can rely on me.' She spread out her left hand and contemplated the squared-off nail-tips. 'I did suggest he took you, but he was adamant you'd hate it.'

Lucy's smile became a little brittle. Only pride kept it there at all. Fionnula knew as well as she did that Dominic hadn't asked her.

As soon as the door closed behind her Lucy pushed the drawing board away angrily. *How she loathed that woman.* And yet Dominic seemed completely unaware of how poisonous she was.

It didn't change anything, though. She didn't need Fionnula to tell her how irreplaceable Eloise was in his life. He'd told her himself.

She looked out into the garden. But Dominic had nearly kissed her.

Now, why was that?

CHAPTER EIGHT

LUCY looked round on hearing her mother's voice.

There was nothing left to do. The hairdresser had been and gone. For once she looked elegant, as if she'd stepped out of a historical portrait. Her hair was dotted with sprays of gypsophila and tiny white rosebuds. No veil, but very bride-like all the same.

'I'll be right there.'

She stood up and reached for her bouquet, a tight posy of apricot roses. Each bloom was perfect and covered with dew-like moisture. A bride's bouquet. *Today she was a bride.* It was impossible not to think about the day she'd done it before. She'd been so hopeful then, with no whisper of the shadow that was to cloud her life.

'You look lovely,' her mother said as soon as Lucy opened the door. 'Let me see the back.' Lucy turned obediently. 'It's a beautiful fit. You've been such a long time I was beginning to worry something was wrong.'

'I'm sorry.'

'Are you nervous, darling?' Lucy didn't need to answer as her mother scarcely paused. 'All brides are, so not to worry,' she said with a gentle stroke on Lucy's cheek. 'That dress is amazing. I love the bodice.'

Lucy looked down at the heavy ivory lace, which was scooped low. It was pretty. It fitted like a second skin and gave way to a sheath-like skirt in rustling apricot covered with fine gauze. 'How do the girls look?'

'Like little poppets,' her mum answered. 'I do wish you'd decided on a church wedding, though, Lucy. It's so much more romantic than the registry office.'

'I've done the church wedding.'

Her mother's face clouded over. 'Yes… I suppose… You haven't rushed into this, have you? Dominic's a lovely man, but there's still time…'

Lucy leant forward and kissed her mother's plump cheek. 'We just wanted it to be different. Dominic's done the big church wedding too. An evening party seemed like a good idea.'

'I suppose so.' She smiled, happy to put her doubts aside. 'No ghosts this way.'

'Exactly.'

And yet there were ghosts everywhere. For her and for Dominic.

When she'd married Michael she'd known he adored her. It had been so exciting, getting ready for their wedding. Looking forward to spending the rest of their lives together. And they'd been very happy—for the short time they'd had.

Today was different. At least she was marrying a man she loved, but Dominic... Every minute of today must be painful for him. Every moment would remind him of just how much he'd lost when Eloise died.

Lucy led the way down the stairs, marvelling at the transformation. The florists who'd fallen on the house with such enthusiasm that morning had wrought a miracle. Dominic had spared no expense in creating a magical backdrop. No wonder her mother was so anxious to believe she'd stumbled into a classic fairytale happy ending.

'I still think we should have sent Dominic somewhere else last night. Auntie Ivy will fall down flat if she ever hears he's seen you on your wedding morning.'

'Well, she's not likely to, is she? It's only going to be you, Jasper and the girls at the register office. Not even Jessie.'

'I'm just old fashioned, I suppose.'

Lucy felt a bit old-fashioned herself. There was something very bizarre about spending the morning in jeans and a T-shirt, discussing with Dominic where it would be best to put the drinks table, before excusing herself to go and put on something a whole lot less comfortable. And now she had to reappear as a bride. *His bride.* She felt absurdly self-conscious as the fabric swished around her legs.

'Here she is,' her mother announced, pushing the door open wide.

Lucy slid miserably in behind her. She would never be Eloise. She could never hope to replace the love of his life.

'You look lovely, Mummy,' Chloe said, putting her hand in Lucy's cold one. 'You look like a princess.'

'You look beautiful,' Dominic said softly, kissing her cheek.

She hadn't realised he'd moved so close. 'Thank you.'

His hand slid lightly down her bare arm and he squeezed her fingers. Instantly, all the emotion she'd been trying to suppress welled up. With shining eyes, she looked up into his calm ones and saw the slight smile he gave her. It was full of tenderness and reassurance. He might not love her, but he did intend to share his life with her. It was worth having. All she had to do was to get through today.

'It's time we were getting to the registry office,' her mother said, gathering up Chloe's posy. 'I don't know where all the time's gone. Abby, pick your flowers up and we'll get in the car.'

Lucy felt numb as everything started to happen around her. She knew Jessie had come and placed a resounding kiss on her cheek and that Dominic's hand rested in the small of her back as he guided her outside. She was bundled in and out of the car, scarcely noticing anything until she stood outside the imposing façade of the register office. It was a dark building. Rather depressing, with huge grey columns either side of a blue-painted door.

'It will be all right,' Dominic said quietly at her elbow.

She struggled to focus her eyes on his face. In evening dress, he was every inch the television personality—successful, wealthy, a man who had everything. Appearances could be so deceptive. Her heart just ached for the sadness he must be feeling. He couldn't really want this.

She smiled. 'I know.'

'This must be difficult for you.'

'For you, too,' she replied, her smile wavering.

He linked his fingers with hers. Slowly he raised them and placed a kiss on her fingers. 'You're cold.'

'Nervous.'

'There's no need. We'll be fine.'

Then the door opened and the whole charade began in earnest. She walked, talked, smiled at all Jasper's fulsome compliments—and felt nothing. Nothing at all.

It was as though everything was happening to someone else. She knew when Abby dropped her posy, saw the registrar arrive in buttercup-yellow and a pair of shoes that made her ankles look thick, heard her mother's gentle clucking as she tried to make the girls stand quietly.

All the time Dominic stood beside her, his hand wrapped securely round hers. She ought to be being more supportive of him. Making more of an effort. When he slid the simple gold band on her finger she tried to smile but it faltered pathetically.

'You may kiss your bride.'

Dominic hesitated for an infinitesimal moment before he allowed his hands to slide up her arms. Lucy felt the air contract around her. They'd practised for this.

The touch of his lips on hers was gentle—loving, even. For this one moment she could allow everything she felt for him to flow through her. *Couldn't she?* It was what was expected of a bride. She closed her eyes and relaxed into his caress. It lasted a handful of seconds at the most, but it sent warmth shimmering through her veins.

When Dominic pulled back she slowly opened her eyes. *They were married.* From this day onwards she was part of his family. It was the beginning. Maybe in time he would come to feel more for her than he did now, but if he didn't...

Well, if he didn't she had two girls to pour her love into. She turned and smiled at them, holding out her hand. 'Come and give me a hug, you two.' She bent down and pulled them in close, her face buried in Abby's hair. It smelt of roses and shampoo. *Her girls.* Chloe and Abby.

Turning to smile up at Dominic, she caught sight of his face. It was bleak. Haunted. Quickly, he turned away and said something to the registrar, but Lucy's tentative happiness faded. There was no hope for the future. She was fooling herself if she allowed herself to dwell on the possibility. His expression had said it all. He was only marrying her because of a tragic mix-up, and every time he looked at her he would remember the pain of that discovery.

The girls chattered, the papers were signed and witnessed and her mother fussed. Lucy could feel her head beginning to ache, but this was only the beginning of a long evening.

'We need to be getting back to the house,' her mother was saying. 'We're running fifteen minutes behind schedule.'

'I'll telephone Jessie and tell her we're on our way,' Jasper said, pulling his mobile phone out of his pocket. 'She's quite capable of keeping the hordes at bay.'

'Ready?' Dominic asked moments later as he came and stood beside her.

Lucy nodded. 'How late are we?'

'Hardly at all. How are you feeling? Any regrets?'

'No.'

'Liar,' he said softly, his fingers lightly touching the side of her face. 'You did very well back there.'

'So did you.' The backs of her eyes began to prickle as she fought to hold back her tears. It was so difficult not to turn her face into the comfort of his hand. But there was no one to see now, no one they had to convince.

Dominic let his hand fall to his side and they walked the short distance to the car in silence. Lucy longed to break it but couldn't think of anything sensible to say. It was as though an immense chasm had opened up between them.

As they approached, the driver leapt to his feet, his face wreathed in smiles. With scarcely a beat Dominic launched himself into a very creditable performance of happy bridegroom. Beside him, Lucy felt awkward and stiff.

'Is this very different from your wedding to Michael?' Dominic asked abruptly as the car purred away.

'Hugely.' She laughed in a valiant effort to lighten the atmosphere between them. 'For a start I insisted on having no photographs and a chocolate wedding cake. We thought we were being very innovative.' The glimmer of amusement in the blue depths of his eyes was reward enough. 'You? Is this very different for you?'

He laughed, his eyes glinting with mischievous amusement. 'Can you imagine what Vanessa's like arranging a wedding? Believe me, this is very different!'

'It must be,' she replied, smiling in response. 'How long do you think everyone will stay this evening?'

'Too long. It doesn't matter much. We'll disappear off as soon as we've had enough.'

Lucy's stomach lurched at the thought of spending a night alone with Dominic. Just the two of them. Without the girls. It was going to feel different, knowing they were alone.

It had all been carefully orchestrated to give the appearance of normality. When Dominic had broached the subject of their wedding night he'd been adamant they shouldn't give anyone grounds for suspicion. His suggestion was that they stay in the Kensington flat of a close friend of his who was working in Dubai. It had two large bedrooms and there'd be no one to question their sleeping arrangements.

She looked across at him. His eyes were closed and his head was laid back on the dark red leather upholstery. The strain of the day was etched on his face. 'Will you tell me when you've had enough?'

'We'll have a secret sign,' he said, opening his eyes and looking at her with the attractive glint that made her tummy turn over. 'Tap your nose three times and I'll whisk you out of there.'

The car drew smoothly up outside Dominic's home.

'Ready?'

This was where she lived now. It still didn't seem possible. How many years would it be before she felt she could offer an opinion on the oversized rhododendrons and suggest they replaced the gravel with something softer? Everywhere she looked she was reminded of Eloise, of the woman whose dreams were expressed in this house.

And there—back in Shropshire—was her home. The one she'd chosen with Michael. Standing empty. At some point she was going to have to make a decision about it. Sell it, maybe? The final link with her past. Pain contracted her chest and she struggled not to cry.

'Do you need to wait a few minutes?' Dominic asked softly at her elbow.

'I'm sorry. It's just…'

'I know.' He smoothed away a single strand of hair falling across her face and anchored it behind one of the roses. 'Everything's happened so quickly. It's going to take some adjusting to. Keep reminding yourself we're in this together. Okay?'

She nodded.

'Let's get this bit over with, then,' he said, leading her up the steps and into the fray.

The immediate impression was one of people—people everywhere. Lucy's eyes swept the room, looking for familiar faces.

'The bride and groom!' Jasper announced loudly.

Dominic leant across and whispered in her ear. 'He's taking his responsibilities very seriously.'

'Lucy—' Abby bounced up to her, ridiculously pretty in her floating dress '—*am* I allowed any of the fruit drink? Grandma George said Chloe and me aren't to have any because it isn't for children.'

'Grandma George?' Lucy clarified, with a quick glance across at Dominic's face. Would he mind his daughter adopting her mother as a grandparent so quickly? Would Vanessa? She could see Eloise's mother standing talking to Fionnula, her expression stormy.

Dominic let go of her hand, saying, 'That's because it's alcoholic. Jessie's made something else you'll like much better.' He smiled across at Lucy. 'Well done, Grandma George! I'll go and sort the girls out. Will you be okay?'

She must have nodded because Dominic disappeared into the throng of people milling about in the doorway, leaving her to make her own way into the room. A small cluster of people to her left smiled and nodded but said nothing as she walked past them.

'Lucy.' Vanessa's cultured voice stopped her.

She turned, already knowing she wasn't going to enjoy this conversation.

'I wanted to speak to you about Abigail. I'm very disappointed she isn't staying with me tonight.'

'I'm sorry—'

'I think as Eloise's mother I have some rights,' the other woman ploughed on in a voice that was slightly slurred.

Lucy drew a deep breath. 'Chloe and Abby wanted to be together tonight. They're very excited. Jessie is staying over to look after them.'

'I know very well she is. She's a very capable woman, but I think I should have been asked. It's what Eloise would have wanted. Even if Dominic has forgotten what he owes to her, I can assure you I haven't.'

Lucy's fingers gripped tightly on her bouquet. 'Both Dominic and I have agreed how important it is for you to have a good relationship with Abby.'

'So we'll consider it settled, then, shall we?' Vanessa said, casting a victorious glance across at Fionnula.

'Abby and Chloe really do want to be together and—'

'And it's quite natural Lucy will want to make changes,' Fionnula cut in as she strolled across to stand beside her aunt. Her voice held all the saccharine sweetness Lucy had come to expect. 'I'm sure she finds it difficult to have Eloise's family so involved with Abby.'

'I won't allow it!'

'Van—'

'I'm going to speak to Dominic. He has a responsibility to my Eloise.' She took another large sip of her wine. 'You may have married him, but you'll find I'm a difficult woman to ignore. I'm Abby's blood relative and I won't allow him to forget that.'

Lucy watched Vanessa march out of the room and felt a pang of sadness at the confrontation Dominic was going to face. She turned to look at Fionnula, taking note of the small, self-satisfied smile hovering about her beautiful mouth. 'I don't intend to deny Vanessa a relationship with her grandchild,' Lucy said softly, trying to defuse the situation.

Fionnula flicked her highly manicured nails. 'Very creditable of you, darling. I don't think you'll have the power to stop it. Dominic is very aware of what he owes to Eloise's memory.'

'And to Abby.'

'Of course,' Fionnula agreed, her eyes scanning the closely packed room. 'I was just having a conversation with someone who was remarking how sensible he'd been to remarry someone maternal rather than try and replace Eloise.'

Lucy felt her anger flicker and then die. This woman had nothing. In the six years since Eloise had died she'd hovered around, hoping to take her cousin's place, but Dominic hadn't looked at her. She was sticking in her little darts of poison, hoping to destroy his marriage before it had even begun. She didn't know there was nothing to spoil. They had a desperate marriage of convenience. Nothing more.

She started as Jasper's voice interrupted. 'Champagne for the bride.'

'Thank you,' she responded, her fingers wrapping around the stem of a tall flute glass.

'Fin, I'm going to have to borrow Lucy. I'm to take her on a tour of duty.' He led her away, whispering, 'I thought you might need rescuing. The wicked witch of the west has collared poor Dom in the kitchen and is slightly the worse for wear from the booze.'

Lucy smiled weakly.

'Uncle Andy! Uncle Andy!' Chloe suddenly swept by in a blur of white organza.

Lucy spun round to see one of Michael's brothers standing in the doorway.

Swinging Chloe effortlessly up into his arms, he came across to her. 'Hello, beautiful,' he said, kissing her cheek. 'I'm the family representative. We couldn't let you do this without someone being here to cheer you along. We're very pleased for you, sweetheart,' he said softly.

Tears welled up inside her. 'I can't believe you're here. I thought you were in the States.'

'I was. The flight was a bit delayed. That's why I'm late.'

'It's so good to see you. I can't believe you're here,' she said again. She looked round for Dominic. 'You must meet Dominic. He's...'

'Right here,' Dominic said at her elbow.

'This is Andrew Grayford, Michael's twin.'

Dominic extended his hand, his eyebrow lifted in surprise. 'Twin?'

'For my sins,' Andrew said, transferring Chloe to his other arm. 'And you're the man who's stolen my sister-in-law.' He smiled. 'We're very pleased for you. The whole family is. Mum really wanted to be here, but it's a long way from Aberdeen and her leg is playing up.'

'I'm so pleased you're here. It's just amazing.'

'Come and meet Abby,' Chloe piped up. 'We're sisters now. And I want to show you my bedroom. It's enormous.'

Andrew lowered her to the floor. 'Lead the way, monkey.' He winked across at Lucy. 'I'll catch you later.'

'I wonder if he'll spot the likeness,' Dominic said softly. 'When he sees Abby.'

'I shouldn't think so. He's not looking for it.'

'No,' he agreed idly. 'Michael was a twin?'

Lucy nodded. 'Identical.' Andy was a shade shorter, but there'd been very little to distinguish between them. She'd forgotten how dark Michael had been, how stocky.

'Is it difficult seeing him?'

She looked back at Dominic. 'Difficult?'

'Does it bring back memories?'

Lucy shook her head and then she smiled. 'I suppose in a way, maybe, but not how you mean. Andrew is Andrew. I'm so glad he came.' It was almost as though Michael had given her his blessing. Her eyes flicked over to Eloise's photograph on the mantelpiece. 'Memories are in your head always.'

He looked away, and then back at her with a swift, twisted smile. 'If Chloe is taking your brother-in-law to meet Abby I ought to go and check Vanessa isn't with her.'

'What did you say to her about tonight?'

'I told her we'd made the arrangements after speaking to the girls.'

His tone was purposeful and brooked no discussion. Lucy felt a pang for the other woman. She must be so frightened of losing the one link she still had with Eloise.

'Jasper—' Dominic turned to address his best man '—keep an eye on Lucy for me while I go and check the girls.'

In fact, he did better than that. Jasper's whispered descriptions of the people she met were wickedly amusing and gradually she found she'd started to relax. With his encouragement, she managed a very creditable tour of duty. Twice she caught sight of Dominic, and once he lifted his glass in a silent toast.

It was almost two hours later before he joined her. She'd ventured as far as the garden terrace, glad to escape the repetitive conversation. The heat of the summer day was beginning to fade and candle lanterns were glowing romantically in the trees. No one would ever imagine it was all an elaborate backdrop for an empty marriage.

'Bearing up?'

'My feet hurt, my face aches from smiling, but other than that...' She smiled. 'It's going all right, isn't it?'

'I think so.' He reached across to the nearby table and picked up another glass of champagne. 'I like Andrew. I had a chat with him.'

'I'm glad,' Lucy replied, uncertain what to say.

'You were right, by the way. He didn't suspect anything when he saw Abby.'

A loud bang ended their conversation.

'Time to cut the cake. Ladies and gentlemen. The cake.' Jasper banged a spoon hard on the table.

Lucy's mother bustled out. 'There you are! You've got a lifetime to talk, you two. It's time to cut the cake.'

Obediently, Dominic led Lucy back through the conservatory and across to the elegant three-tiered confection. It was simply iced and decorated with edible flowers, mainly white but dotted with shades of apricot. With Dominic's arm encircling her waist, she turned to smile into the camera. She felt his hand cover hers as together they cut through the rich fruit cake.

'Kiss the bride!'

'Yes, kiss the bride,' another voice echoed.

Lucy felt her heart lurch. Dominic's hand stilled on hers and then he kissed her. Around her she could hear the cheers but they didn't matter. Everything faded away and she was only aware of him, the taste of him, the feel of his jacket beneath her fingers.

Drawing back, he rested his forehead on hers, before kissing it lightly. Then, linking his fingers through hers, he led her back out into the garden. 'Shall we go?'

'Now?'

He touched his nose three times. 'We can slip away now. No one will notice.'

Lucy suddenly felt nervous. 'But Chloe? Abby? We ought to say goodbye.'

'I've done it. They're with Jessie and your mother. I said we'd disappear as soon as we'd cut the cake and we didn't want a fuss.'

There was nothing left to do then. 'Right,' she said, lifting her chin with determination. 'We'd better get changed.'

'Do you need a hand?'

'No.' She shook her head vigorously. They walked in silence up to the swimming pool and unlocked the door. 'It was a good idea to leave a change of clothes in here. We'd have never managed to leave without being spotted other-wise.'

'Did Vanessa upset you?' he asked from the cubicle next door.

Lucy unzipped the side seam, pulling the dress over her head. 'It's a difficult day for her.' She hung the dress carefully on a hanger, her fingers shaking slightly. 'Where was Cyril? I didn't see him anywhere.' It was so strange to be having a conversation with Dominic whilst standing in a lacy bra and panties.

'He didn't come.'

Lucy's hand hesitated on her red sundress. 'Because of me? I'm so sorry.'

She could almost feel him shrug. 'It's not your fault.'

And it wasn't. All they'd done was make the best of an impossibly difficult situation. She suddenly felt overwhelmingly tired. It washed over her in an unstoppable tide.

In that moment, everything seemed hopeless. She was the wife of a man who couldn't love her and, deep down, she knew she deserved more. She didn't want so very much in life. It wasn't unreasonable to want someone to love and be loved by.

Lucy slipped her arms through the straps of her dress and reached round for the zip. It was too late now. She—*they*—were going to have to make the best of it. How was he feeling now?

'Are you done?'

Lucy quickly pulled up the last bit of the zip and opened the door. 'All ready. Oh, except the hair. I forgot to take the flowers out. That's going to look a bit daft.'

'Come here.' Dominic smiled. Deftly, he began to take out the tiny blooms.

She stood still.

'They've lasted really well.'

'I suppose it was only a few hours,' she said, holding her hand out for the flowers he'd removed.

His blue eyes glinted down at her. 'It seems longer.'

'Did you hate it?'

'Pretty much all of the time. How about you?'

'Not as much as I'd expected. It was good of Andy to come. It was nice of him to travel such a long way.' She was gabbling, she knew. She couldn't seem to stop it. He was so tall, so close. 'And the girls really enjoyed it all, didn't they?'

'The girls are happy.'

Lucy flicked her eyes up nervously as she caught an edge to his voice. His face was centimetres from hers, his fingers gently pulling on her hair as he released the gypsophila from the tiny plaits that held them in place. 'I'm sorry Cyril didn't feel able to come. It must make it hard for you.' Her voice sounded breathless and she bit down on her lip.

His hand stilled for a second. 'As long as he didn't upset you. He's got no idea of the sacrifice you're making,' he said, taking out the last of the flowers.

'You too,' she managed on a whisper.

Slowly, his hand stroked down the side of her face, his thumb caressing her cheekbone. Lucy held her breath, afraid to move. It was a moment of infinite tenderness. She searched his eyes, her own asking a question she couldn't put words to.

And then he turned away—the moment had passed.

'I left my car on the road outside. I didn't want to risk getting blocked in or having Jasper decorate it for me.'

'I hadn't thought of that.' She let the flowers fall to the floor and reached round for her handbag. His precious Morgan decorated with balloons and a 'Just Married' banner would have been the height of absurdity. 'I imagine Jasper enjoys that kind of thing.'

'You could say that.'

Lucy looked at him questioningly.

'When I married Eloise he put a fish in the air conditioning. The car reeked for weeks until we worked out where the smell was coming from.' He led the way behind the summerhouse and out through the garden gate. 'We should be all right. I didn't trust him with the keys this time,' he said, glancing down at her.

Lucy smiled dutifully. Expensive and individual, Dominic's car was yet another echo of Eloise. Dominic's late wife had ordered the Morgan as a surprise. By the time his name was at the top of the waiting list she'd already been dead five years. She didn't need Dominic to tell her; Fionnula's snippets of information were embedded in her head.

The heel of her shoe caught on a raised edge of paving and she stumbled.

'Steady.' His hand shot out and stayed, warm, against the small of her back. 'Everyone will think you've had too much champagne.'

Lucy forced herself to laugh. 'I think they'll guess I'm just not elegant enough for heels.'

'I doubt that,' he said, holding open the car door. 'But it's strange having you reach higher than my shoulder.'

She settled herself in the seat and let her head fall back on the rest. *Had Eloise been higher than his shoulder?* That was something Fionnula hadn't told her.

Dominic climbed into the driving seat beside her, shutting the door with a bang.

'Does Jessie have the telephone number of where we are?' she asked suddenly, turning to look at him.

'Of course. I don't think I've forgotten anything. All we have to do now is convince everyone we've had a wonderful wedding night and then they'll hopefully leave us to get on with it.'

The edge to his voice was unmistakable. She could hear the tension in it, the longing for this whole façade to be over. Her heart ached for him. Was he thinking about his last honeymoon? *Venice.* They'd been to Venice. Fionnula had made sure she knew as though it would underline the fact she was a second-best wife.

He drove in silence, expertly manoeuvring his way through the busy streets. She let her head fall sideways so she could look at him. It seemed incredible she'd only known him for a few short weeks. He was a part of her now.

And this was their wedding night—in a borrowed flat in Kensington.

CHAPTER NINE

'IT MAY well smell a bit musty. Oliver's been away for four months,' Dominic said as he opened the front door.

He stood back to allow Lucy to walk in first. Trendy sisal flooring ran the length of the hall, the walls were bare and the overwhelming impression was of a place closed and shut up. It seemed fitting for an empty honeymoon.

Dominic threw open a door to a small bedroom and put his overnight bag on the bed. 'I thought I'd have this one and give you the main one,' he said over his shoulder. 'It's got the *en suite* bathroom.'

'Whichever.' She pulled her arms closely about her. 'I don't mind.'

'I'll carry your case through.'

Still hovering in the doorway, Lucy stepped back to allow him to pass.

'There's not much cupboard space, I'm afraid, because Oliver's obviously left his stuff here.'

'How long is he away for?'

Dominic lifted her bag on to the king-sized bed of the opposite room. 'A couple more months. There,' he said, turning round to look at her. 'I'll go and open a bottle of wine. It's far too early to go to bed yet.'

She could feel the blood rush to her face, even though she knew he didn't mean that the way it sounded. Nervously, she looked down at her watch. 'It's only nine. It feels so much later.'

'We had a busy morning.'

'Poor Jessie. I hope she manages okay.'

Dominic strode across the bedroom and flung open the far door. 'The *en suite* bathroom is here,' he said unnecessarily.

She nodded.

'Right, I'll leave you to get settled and go and see to that wine.'

As soon as he'd left, Lucy sat down and covered her face with her hands, embarrassment coursing through her. She had to get herself under control. She had to stop reminding herself this was supposed to be her wedding night and forget all the connotations that brought.

'Red or white?' His voice echoed down the hallway.

Lucy leapt to her feet, startled. 'Your choice. I don't mind,' she called back, wrenching open her case quickly in case he returned.

On the top lay the apricot silk negligée Jessie had bought her as a wedding gift. It was beautiful. Soft and sensuous. She hadn't had the heart to leave it behind at the house in case Jessie found it. Lucy let her fingers run over the shimmering fabric. It was what a bride should wear on her wedding night. It was sexy and romantic.

'I've gone for a red,' he called again.

Lucy rolled the negligée up in a tight ball and stuffed it under the nearest pillow. She wasted a few minutes pulling the pins out of her hair and carefully folded her towel across the rail. Anything to delay the moment when she'd have to join Dominic in the lounge. She felt so absurdly self-conscious.

In the end there was nothing left to do.

Dominic looked up as she entered. 'We'd better drink to us,' he said, handing her a large, full glass.

Her hand shook slightly as she took it from him. 'To us,' she agreed obediently, taking a sip. 'This is gorgeous.'

'I brought it from home.'

'Oh.'

'There's nothing much on television. I should have thought about it earlier and hired a video.'

Lucy perched on one of the sofas, her eyes flicking nervously about the room. 'I do like this lounge. It's got a nice feel.'

'I wouldn't have thought it bright enough for you.'

'I like houses to be comfortable. To look like you needn't worry about putting down your mug. You know, not too perfect—' She broke off.

'Unlike my house?'

'I didn't mean...'

Dominic smiled sadly, sitting down opposite her. 'It's all right. I already know you wouldn't choose to live like...' He flicked a glance across at her. 'Like Eloise.'

Silence stretched between them. Lucy fidgeted in her seat and traced her finger around the rim of the glass.

'You're very different.'

'Yes,' she said helplessly.

'Appearances mattered to her.'

Lucy took another sip of wine and waited. She watched as he slowly untied his laces and eased his feet out of his shoes. His face was etched with exhaustion.

He leant back and rubbed the back of his neck. 'The house was a stage-set, really. When she couldn't have children she poured herself into designing the house.' He sipped at his wine, letting the rich, heavy flavours roll about his tongue.

Lucy waited.

'I just let it happen around me. She hired Joseph Finchingly and I agreed to all their plans.'

'It's a beautiful house.'

He drank again and then reached for the bottle, topping up his glass before offering it to her. Lucy shook her head.

'It's very like her. Beautiful, controlled and organised.'

'You must miss her,' she said softly, her hands cradled about her wine glass. It was difficult to sit and listen to him. Eloise had been so perfect, so impossible to compete with. How could anyone hope to compete with a ghost? And yet he so rarely spoke about her she felt compelled to listen.

'I do. Did,' he corrected, bringing his eyes back into focus on Lucy. 'You know, sometimes I feel so bloody guilty. In the beginning...' He paused, swirling the dark red liquid in his glass. 'In the beginning I couldn't sleep because every time I closed my eyes I could see her. Going to sleep was worse. For a few fantastic moments when I woke I'd think everything was okay and then it would all come crashing down around me. That horrible sense of loss and longing...but you must understand that.'

Lucy murmured something incomprehensible. She understood everything he was saying, and yet for Dominic it must have been so much worse.

Michael had been ill and his death hadn't been unexpected. When it had come it had actually been a relief. Loving him as she'd done, she hadn't wanted him to live on in such pain. For Dominic, Eloise's death had come abruptly. One day they'd been ecstatically looking forward to the new life about to join them and the next it had been over. She could only imagine how he had felt.

Dominic stood abruptly and turned on a table lamp and the light pooled around it. 'I shouldn't be talking about this.'

'Why?' Lucy kicked off her heels and curled into the corner of the sofa. The dusky light was intimate and comforting. 'Sometimes it helps to talk.'

He shrugged and sat back down. For a minute or so there was silence. 'I don't remember very much about those first few days after she died. Other people took over everything. Looked after Abby.' He looked at her, his eyes haunted. 'I didn't even give her a name. Not in the beginning. Eloise and I had talked about it, of course, but we hadn't made our final decision. She wanted to look at our baby and decide then.'

Dominic leant forward and held his head in his hands. Every line of his body conveyed sorrow. Lucy longed to reach out and touch him. To comfort him somehow. But she didn't have that right—all she could do was offer him empathy.

'I did that,' she said softly. 'Michael said, ''a baby is a baby,'' but I looked at Chloe when she was minutes old and knew she couldn't be called anything else.'

Dominic looked directly at her, his resonant voice pooling in the silence. 'I let Eloise down even with that. I think I almost hated Abby when I first saw her. She was red and wrinkled—angry as hell—and I didn't know what to do with her.'

Lucy put her drink down on the low side table and got up to kneel at his feet. 'It doesn't—'

'I'd never held a baby.' He pulled a hand through his hair. 'Eloise had bought everything, read the books, got the nursery ready. I'd just assumed I'd eventually get the hang of it. The whole baby thing had been something she'd wanted. All the way through the pregnancy I tried to pretend it wasn't really happening in case something went wrong.' He stopped and took another long sip of wine. 'I was right about that, wasn't I?'

'Is that when Jessie came?'

He nodded, leaning back on the sofa, watching her. 'That was my bright idea. I thought I could buy someone to take away my responsibility. It didn't work, though. Abby wasn't very easy to ignore. And then I had to give her a name. I'd run out of time and everyone was fed up of calling her ''the baby''.'

'So you called her Abigail because it meant ''father rejoiced''.' He looked surprised. 'You told me,' she said, her voice husky. Whether it was the wine or the night talking, Dominic was opening up before her eyes. Letting her see some of the pain that tortured his soul. 'It's probably why I agreed to marry you. I thought if you'd done that for Abby, when it was most difficult, you had to be a good man.'

He laughed harshly. 'Don't make a saint out of me. It was a momentary impulse.'

'But a good one.'

He took a gulp of wine. 'I don't know where it came from. I'd been left to manage. She was so tiny and vulnerable, and I knew I didn't want her to blame herself. Not the way I was going to have to for the rest of my life.'

Lucy leant forward earnestly. 'Why blame? It doesn't have to be anyone's fault.'

'You don't understand.'

'No, I don't.' Lucy shook her head vehemently, the light from the lamp illuminating all the natural colours in her hair.

'I killed her.'

'No.'

'If I'd refused to go ahead with the IVF she'd still be living.'

Lucy touched his knee tentatively. 'You can't say that. Eloise had a heart problem? Right?'

He nodded.

'You can't possibly imagine what may or may not have happened. Her condition might have worsened as she got older, even without a pregnancy.' She hesitated as she searched for the right words. 'Besides, I don't think it actually matters. Not really.'

Dominic's eyes were fixed on her face, his body still.

'Eloise wanted to have a baby. It's a natural urge for some women. Unstoppable. They'd do anything to have one.' She paused again, before continuing quietly. 'I know what that feels like. I was thinking about everything last night.' She sighed. 'I don't know if I can explain it properly, but I suddenly realised I wouldn't change anything even if I could.'

'Nothing?'

'It's been painful and difficult, but I think Abby and Chloe are worth it. We're so very lucky to have them in our lives. And I think…' She hesitated, uncertain whether she should actually say the words. 'I think Eloise and Michael would feel the same.'

He swirled his wine in his glass, his mind back in the past. Eloise had known the risks when she went ahead with the IVF and she'd still decided to take them. He'd been weaker;

he'd decided to pretend they didn't exist. But if he'd really thought about it he would have tried harder to persuade her that their life was full enough anyway. *He should have done that.*

'You're a historian. You ought to know that countless women over the centuries have made the choice to save the life of their baby rather than themselves. It's kind of the same, isn't it?'

He drained the last of his wine. 'She died, Lucy. She died because of me.' His voice sounded weary.

Lucy shook her head again. 'She died because she had a heart problem. It's different.'

'I promised I'd never forget her.'

'And you haven't—'

Dominic put his empty glass down on the side. 'Before I knew anything about the mix-up, before any of this…I was trying to tell Abby about her mother. And I couldn't remember.' His eyes were dark. She'd never seen them look so haunted. 'I can look at a photograph and I can describe what I see. I can remember what she achieved, some of the things we did—but everything's starting to fade. When I close my eyes now I don't see her. I can't picture what she would have done with Abby. How it would have been.'

Lucy reached for his hand and curved her own about it. 'That's sad—but it's natural, I think. I can't imagine what Michael would have been like as a father if he hadn't been sick. It wasn't what happened. We have to make the best of it.'

Dominic reached out and stroked the side of her face. 'You don't understand, Lucy. I promised myself I wouldn't ever forget her. I wouldn't let anyone else replace her—ever.'

The words struck steel through Lucy's heart. It was what she'd expected, had known, after all. He'd explained that very carefully to her at the beginning. He didn't intend to love again.

'I know,' she whispered.

'Do you? Then why do I want to do this?' he asked, leaning forward and running his thumb across her lips. 'And why do I want to do this?' His hand cradled the back of her head and his lips came down on hers. Almost angry. She could feel the way he was fighting his response to her and yet he couldn't help himself any more than she could. His body softened and his kiss became giving.

He leant back and looked at her passion-filled eyes. 'Why do I want to do that, Lucy?'

Lucy didn't know what to say. She wanted to tell him how much she loved him but knew he didn't want to hear it. Above everything else, she wanted to make everything all right for him. She wanted to heal his pain. Make him feel ready to go on with living in all its fullness.

She licked her lips nervously. 'I don't know. Perhaps because we're in the same boat. We've got the girls...'

'You think it's just because we've been thrown together?' His fingers moved across her hair, stroking gently.

'It's possible,' she began, and then she could say no more. She was in his arms being kissed. Not gently, but passionately, as though he couldn't help himself. He wanted her close and then closer still.

And that was what she wanted. She pressed herself up against his body and kissed him back, revelling in the chance to touch him.

'Lucy—' he broke off painfully. 'I can't promise you anything. I can't—'

She pressed her fingers against his lips and stopped him. 'I understand. Just for tonight, let's forget. Let's forget there's anyone but us.'

He groaned and his lips pressed against hers fervently. 'I don't want to be alone tonight. For tonight?' He held her back to look into her face, his eyes raking hers, looking for the answer he wanted.

Inwardly, Lucy groaned. *Just for tonight?* Could she convince him she wanted just one night with him when actually she wanted the whole fairytale? The one her mother believed she was living. She wanted to live with him, love him and grow old with him. 'Just for to-night.'

It was what he wanted to hear. She could feel the tension leave his body as he gave himself over to other sensations. Lucy felt almost giddy with delirium as she felt him lift her up and carry her through to the bedroom. She had to remember this. Every second. She had to score it deep into her memory and keep it with her always. Every sensation, every thought, every feeling.

She tried to remember the coolness of the sheet as he laid her gently down. How it felt when he smoothed back her hair from her face and kissed her as though she were the only woman in his world. How it felt when he slid down the narrow straps of her sundress. And then she couldn't remember any more. It all blurred together into a mix of scents, of feeling, of movement and, at the last, a kaleidoscopic burst of colour.

This was more than she'd ever hoped to experience with him. More than she'd dreamed possible when she'd agreed to this marriage. If this was the only night they were going to have together then it was still worth everything.

She gave herself up to the moment, amazed when she heard her own voice shout out. His arms held her safely. It was so beautiful. So unbelievably beautiful. Emotion welled up deep inside her and spilled out on her cheek.

'Did I hurt you?' Dominic asked softly, his finger wiping away the tear.

Lucy shook her head but she couldn't speak; there weren't words to put to what she was feeling. She'd promised not to say them anyway.

She felt his lips gently kiss her hair and he turned her so he could cradle her body against his. 'Sleep now.'

And Lucy did. She could feel the steady beat of his heart against her back and his breath in her hair. She would never forget how this felt. How incredibly wonderful it was. She let her heavy limbs relax and her eyes close.

*　　*　　*

Lucy woke as the morning light filtered through the wooden blinds and knew she was alone.

'Dominic?' she called softly, not really expecting an answer. She reached out and ran her hand across cold cotton. He was already up.

She stretched languorously. After last night it was no wonder she'd overslept. It had been the fulfilment of a dream. So much more than she'd dared to let herself hope for.

It had been perfect. Excitement coursed through her veins and anticipation settled in her stomach. For years she hadn't let herself hope for the best, and yet suddenly anything seemed possible.

'Lucy?' Dominic's voice called softly from the other side of the bedroom door.

She sat up and pulled the sheet up with her. Foolish, after all they'd shared, to feel so shy. 'Y-Yes?'

'Are you ready for a cup of tea?'

Lucy ran a hand through her tangled curls. 'Th-that would be lovely.'

The door slowly opened and Dominic walked in, fully clothed and holding a steaming mug.

'How long have you been up?'

'A while.'

'You should have woken me.' Lucy watched him closely, the first sense of unease piercing her happiness. Something was wrong.

He put the mug down on a slate coaster and turned away. 'I've made breakfast, when you're ready. We shouldn't be too late getting back to the girls.'

The truth thumped through her. *He couldn't look at her.* Lucy clutched at the sheet, too afraid to speak. Why couldn't he look at her?

As he reached the door he hesitated, one hand resting on the doorframe. 'Lucy, I—'

She waited, her heart slamming against her ribcage.

'I…just wanted to say…thank you.'

And then he closed the door, the click as final as the tone of his voice. Lucy took her quivering bottom lip firmly between her teeth. She wasn't stupid enough to need to ask what he'd been thanking her for. *And he hadn't been able to look at her.*

They'd agreed it was for one night only. For comfort. Lucy wanted to scream. She ripped the sheet off her with furious energy. Just when she thought she'd become acclimatised to hell another door opened and she realised there was just room after room of unimaginable agony.

And she felt foolish. She should have realised when she woke alone that something was wrong. Perhaps his 'thank you' was just politeness. He didn't look thankful. He looked like a man who was hoping the floor would open and swallow him whole.

She turned on the shower and waited while it reached the correct temperature. He so obviously regretted what had passed between them it was humiliating. But *why*? Why regret something so perfect? Hadn't he felt the connection between them? The rightness of their being together?

Obviously not.

Lucy let the water cascade over her cold body. He hadn't made love to her. He'd used her for comfort and allowed her to use him. Just as they'd agreed. But she hadn't needed comfort. What she wanted from him was love. She wanted to have him love her and be allowed to love him.

Lucy dressed quickly in her red sundress, trying to ignore the memory of how it had felt when he'd pushed aside the spaghetti straps and pressed kisses in the hollow of her shoulder. She hadn't imagined the way his eyes had burned into hers. The way he'd said her name. So why was he doing this now?

She had to know what he was thinking. This wasn't a relationship she could just walk away from. She was committed to a marriage. She was going to see him day after day, year after year. Did he regret sleeping with her because of Eloise? Was it guilt? Did he feel he'd betrayed his late wife? And, if so, where did that leave her now?

Pausing only to pick up her mug, she followed the sounds coming from the kitchen. She had to speak to him, even though it was obvious he didn't want that.

'Do you want bacon?' Dominic asked without turning round.

'Er—I think so.'

'How many rashers?'

'Two will be fine.' She needed him to turn round, to look at her.

'How do you like your eggs?'

This was beginning to make her angry. She deserved better than this. Why wouldn't he look at her? 'I've no idea. As they come.'

'One or—?'

'One is plenty.' She cut him off. She was going to have to speak to him now, before she lost her nerve. 'Dominic, about what—'

'I know.' And then he turned round. His eyes were bleak and she had her answer. It was more painful than a physical blow would have been. It struck at the very core of her and left a mark she'd never be rid of. 'It probably wasn't a good idea.'

'Wh—?'

'Changing the rules.'

It was unbelievably painful. She'd never really known rejection—not like this. Dominic was the second man she'd ever made love to. Just the second. A hard lump settled in the back of her throat, making it impossible to swallow, let alone speak. She wanted to find a way of breaking through the barrier he'd erected round himself. Make him tell her how he felt about Eloise. About her. Without that communication there was no hope for anything better. But she couldn't do it.

'I haven't forgotten what we agreed.'

Her mouth moved soundlessly.

'I know yesterday was difficult—' he looked down at his shoes '—for both of us. Too much emotion…'

'Yes,' she agreed helplessly. There was nothing else to say.

Dominic turned back and flicked her egg on to a plate. 'I've rung Jessie and told her we'll be back before ten.'

'Good.'

He passed her breakfast across to her. 'I'm sorry, Lucy. I—'

'Nothing broken,' she said with a passable attempt at a shrug. 'It'll be good to get back to the girls.'

Did he know she loved him? Was that why he was apologising? She couldn't let him see how broken she felt. He couldn't have made it plainer that he thought last night was a mistake. But, dear God, it hadn't been. Not for her. What was she going to do? How could she live through this?

There was going to be no escape. She couldn't just pretend it hadn't happened. She was going to have to live with Dominic, knowing he bitterly regretted going to bed with her.

CHAPTER TEN

Lucy closed her studio door with relief on Jessie's constant chatter. Getting caught with a bundle of bedding from the annexe hadn't been the best start to the day. If Jessie knew she slept downstairs every night she hadn't said so, but there was little doubt that she was beginning to question the notion of a conscientious artist working late into the night. Some time soon she was going to start asking some awkward questions.

Actually, Lucy hadn't done much painting since the girls had gone back to school. Not as much as she'd hoped. She was always so tired, with the kind of exhaustion that seemed to seep into your bones too deeply for sleep to work properly. It was similar to how she'd felt after Michael had died—listless and lacking concentration.

But then the past weeks had been difficult, and she was as lonely as she'd been back then. The girls were away all day, she'd no good friends in London yet, and Dominic was more distant than ever. He was unfailingly polite, but she knew he avoided her company whenever possible. Instead of bringing them closer together, their night of lovemaking had driven a huge wedge between them. Since that first miserable morning they'd never spoken about it. Sometimes she wondered whether it was all in her imagination—the tenderness and passion of that night.

She sat on the stool and looked at where she'd got to with her landscape. Gently, she wet the watercolour with a moist brush and mixed a cool purple with a little Alizarin crimson for the shadows of St Paul's Cathedral. Her teeth bit her lip in concentration as she painted in the purple shadow, allowing patches of the earthy wash to show through.

She didn't hear the door open behind her, and Dominic's voice came as a shock. He so rarely intruded into what he regarded as her space. 'Do you mind if I go to Northumberland a few days earlier than planned?'

Lucy put down the brush and turned to look at him. 'Of course not.' He looked tired. Smudges darkened the skin under his eyes and he didn't seem to smile any more. Was he as miserable as she was?

'Fionnula's just telephoned to say she's booked rooms for us for tonight. It makes sense to start up north and work our way back to London. We're committed to Essex on Thursday week, so it would be better to do Northumberland sooner rather than later.'

Lucy turned back, methodically loading her brush with a touch of ultramarine blue. 'It's half-term next week. The girls will miss you.'

His mouth twisted. 'I doubt they'll even notice I'm gone. I hardly saw anything of them last weekend.'

It was an abrupt change of plan. A sudden suspicion entered her mind. 'Did Jessie tell you she's going away next week?'

He hesitated. 'She mentioned it yesterday evening. Does that make any difference?'

'Not really,' she answered with a grim smile. Why was she surprised? It made sense of why he'd give up time with the girls. 'When will you go?'

'After lunch.' He went to leave, and then stopped. 'If you want to arrange some time for yourself at the beginning of November, I'll make sure I'm here to take over the girls.'

'I'm fine. We'll be fine.' She added the blue to the shadows. 'Leave contact numbers for me on the side in the kitchen and I'll see you when you get back.'

'Right.' His hand hesitated on the door handle. 'Lucy?'

She turned to look at him.

'Are—?' Dominic broke off and gave a slight shake of the head. 'It's nothing. I'll see you when I get back.'

As soon as he'd gone, Lucy put the brush down. It hurt so much. Dominic could scarcely manage to stay in the same room with her now. For all their unwillingness to express it, they both knew his need to go away tonight had less to do with work and more to do with his desire to escape. This was the third time since their wedding he'd found an excuse to go away. How long would they be able to go on pretending?

Automatically, she picked up her brush again and rinsed out the bristles before leaving it to dry. It didn't help either to have Fionnula hovering about all the time, her sharp eyes watching and judging the state of their marriage. She was like a huge spider waiting to pounce.

Putting her stool neatly under the desk, Lucy turned towards the small bedroom as tiredness overwhelmed her. Wearily, she kicked off her shoes and lay down on the mattress, pulling the duvet over her.

At some point they were going to have to accept their marriage had been a mistake. She was dying inside every day she spent in this relationship. Although to call what she shared with Dominic a relationship was ridiculous. She lived in his house, cared for Abby and Chloe. He'd suggested it for honourable reasons, but it just wasn't enough that they both loved the girls. They weren't a *family*. They shared the girls now as though they were already divorced. Nothing much would change.

Divorced. She let the word roll about her head as she drifted into sleep. Could she be brave enough to let Dominic go? Could she face a future where she'd never see him again over breakfast or hear his deep voice reading their girls a story? Could she accept the fact he'd never be able to love her and that the greatest gift she could give him would be his freedom?

She woke feeling a dark net had been closed over her, that she was being pulled away from something precious. She was clawing at the nylon strings and too frightened to scream.

Lucy sat up and rubbed at her face before glancing down at her wristwatch. She'd slept for over two hours! She couldn't believe it. This wasn't like her at all. Perhaps this was depression and she ought to go and see her doctor? She caught sight of herself in the bedroom mirror. Certainly she looked depressed. Her face was sallow and her eyes no longer sparkled. She couldn't go on like this—and neither could Dominic.

'Jessie?' she called, coming out of the studio.

'Dominic's already left. He said not to disturb you,' Jessie said, lifting a cake out of the oven.

Lucy pulled the elastic band out of her hair. She had the house to herself again. It should be a relief to know she didn't have to creep around, worrying she was disturbing him. No more of those awkward silences.

'Fionnula was here.' Jessie sniffed. Lucy could hear the disapproval in her voice. The older woman didn't trust Fionnula, perhaps with good reason. Jessie turned round to hang up the oven gloves. 'She means mischief, that one.'

'They work together,' Lucy said wearily, sitting on a high stool.

'For a clever man, he's a fool. Fionnula's invested far too many years to let go easily. Now he's married he ought to put a stop to her silly games.'

Lucy picked up a spoon and began to stir the sugar in the nearby bowl. She felt too tired to fight, too hurt. She'd never felt so weak or so buffeted before.

'Have you told him about the baby?'

Lucy looked up, shocked. 'I'm not. I—'

'I've looked after more households while a woman was having a baby than you've had hot dinners.'

'Jessie,' Lucy began, her mind too amazed to formulate the words properly, 'I can't... Chloe's an IVF baby. We couldn't...'

'That's as may be,' she said stoutly, turning back to ease her cake out of the tin. 'But was it you or Michael who couldn't? You may call me a fool if I'm wrong. There's no reason I know of why Dominic can't father a quiverful of children. Maybe you two ought to be a bit more careful.'

Pregnant?

It wasn't possible—and yet the tiredness, the tearfulness, the missed period, the way her body felt different. *A baby?*

Jessie set the cake on a cooling tray and took the tin across to the sink. 'It's just what the pair of you need. A baby to pull the family together.'

'Jessie, I—'

'Do a test and then don't take too long in telling Dominic.' She wiped her hands and smiled. 'I'd pay big money to see Fionnula's face.'

A baby? Lucy sat numb. She was too scared to believe it was possible. It was what she'd wanted all her adult life. No medical intervention. Just a man and a woman creating a life together.

Slowly, a single tear began to fall down her cheek. Was it really possible she was going to have Dominic's baby?

'Lucy?'

Lucy looked up into Jessie's concerned face and sniffed. 'I'm all right. It's just I didn't let myself believe it was possible. It's...'

'I know, it's always an emotional time having a baby. Dominic won't find it easy, of course, what with Eloise dying as she did. It's going to bring back some difficult memories for him.' She turned round and reached for a chopping board. 'Why don't you go and have a nice shower to freshen you up after your nap while I make us some soup. Is courgette and potato all right?'

'I'm not very hungry,' she said, distracted.

'But you'll need to eat something.'

'Yes. I suppose…' Lucy slipped down from the stool.

Pregnant. She didn't really doubt it was true. Now Jessie had said it she recognised the signs for herself. She was going to have Dominic's baby. It was a miracle. And yet…

She walked into the lounge and picked up the picture of Eloise. She was so beautiful. Irreplaceable. Lucy's mouth twisted in pain as she looked down into the face of the woman Dominic loved. A woman too perfect to compete with. If Eloise had loved him as much as he had her she wouldn't have wanted him to live out the rest of his life with a woman he couldn't love. And neither did she.

But a baby changed everything. *What was she going to do now?*

Lucy placed the picture back on the mantelpiece and hugged her arms tightly about her body. Could she spend the rest of her life knowing he loved their children but could never love her, that he regretted the night that had brought this life into being?

As soon as Dominic knew about the baby he would never let her go, however unhappy he was with her. But what was the alternative? She couldn't lie to him and pretend she was pregnant by someone else. She couldn't do that to him or to the baby. *It was such a mess.* How could fate be so cruel as to make the most wonderful thing happen to her at the worst possible time?

Lucy pulled her hand across her eyes. She needed to think and she couldn't do it here. Not in Eloise's house with all her things about her. She'd give anything to be at home. Just the thought of her terraced home made her feel desperately homesick. She even missed the spiders.

And there was nothing to stop her—for a couple of weeks, at least. She could take the girls for half-term and borrow a few extra days. A simple phone call to Dominic and she could be home by the weekend. And then, she promised herself, she'd make some serious decisions about her future—their future.

'Jessie,' she called, walking back down the long hallway. 'I'm going for a walk.'

'But your lunch—'

'I know. I'll get something while I'm out.' She reached for her black coat, slipping in her arms and pulling the belt tight. 'I'll collect the girls from school on my way home.'

A baby! She was going to have Dominic's baby.

Lucy wandered about the wide London streets, aware of nothing very much. She made one stop at the local chemist and bought the pregnancy test that would confirm what she already knew.

It was just good to be out of the house. Everything had changed when she had realised she loved him. It had changed again after they'd made love. She couldn't forget the expression in his eyes as he'd held his body over hers. It had been pride, exultation—almost *love*. But it had been an illusion. He'd used her for comfort and he'd allowed her to use him. Nothing more—just as they'd agreed.

Just for one night.

She'd been stupid to believe she could shut off her emotions like that. She was the faithful kind, the 'till death us do part' kind of girl.

Lucy did the school pick-up on auto-pilot, acutely conscious of the pregnancy test in her pocket. *Dominic's baby*. At least she had one night to remember. One precious, perfect evening. She'd never forget it. But his daily rejection of her hurt every day. Could she live with that?

'When's Daddy coming home?'

She took hold of Abby's hand. 'As soon as he can, sweetheart. You know we'll all be very proud of him when he's on the television.'

'I don't like castles.'

'No?' Lucy licked her lips nervously. This was difficult. If it had been hard explaining to the girls why Dominic had gone away without saying goodbye, how much harder would it be to explain why they didn't want to be married any more? 'I was wondering whether we could go to Shropshire while he's away. You could see where Chloe and I used to live.'

'Yes!' Chloe shouted. 'There's a big wood right behind our house and you can sleep in my room.'

'Can I?' Abby let go of Lucy's hand.

Lucy pushed her hands into her coat pockets as she watched the girls kicking leaves along the grey London pavement. *She had to go home*. All she needed to do now was telephone Dominic and tell him where she'd be.

And that was difficult enough. Lucy waited until the girls were asleep. It was near enough eight-thirty by then, and the house was so quiet. She sat in her studio, hands cradled around a mug of coffee and her eyes fixed on the silver handset. It would have been easier if she could have built up her courage with a large glass of wine but she couldn't—not now.

The pregnancy test sat on the side, unopened. That was for the morning. She couldn't speak to Dominic tonight *knowing for sure* and not telling him. This way she bought herself a little more time. But she still had to speak to him. Hear his voice.

Lucy carefully unfolded the sheet of paper Dominic had left her. Her hand shook as she keyed out the number and asked for him in Room Seventy-two.

'I'm sorry, Dom isn't here at the moment. Can I help at all?'

There was no mistaking the sexily smooth voice of Fionnula. Lucy had been so worked up at the prospect of speaking to Dominic she almost didn't know what to do. 'It's Lucy. Wh-when will he be back?'

'I can give him a message. Would you like him to phone you?'

'P-please.'

'It would probably be better if he rings you. He hates to be disturbed when he's working.'

Lucy made small circles with her finger on the beechwood coffee table. Fionnula was hateful. She knew that. It changed nothing. All she had to do was tell Dominic where he could find them—where he could find the girls. 'Can you say I'm going home?'

'Of course, darling.' Fionnula's laugh tinkled down the line. 'We're having supper tonight. I'll tell him then. Do you plan on staying long?'

Lucy got up. 'I—I don't really know. Just tell him to ring me in Shropshire if he wants to speak to the girls.' She didn't wait for Fionnula to answer before replacing the handset in the cradle as though it had burnt her.

She looked down at her wrist-watch. Eight-forty was late for supper. It made it sound romantic and intimate. But that was what Fionnula had intended.

It didn't matter. All that mattered was that she'd done what she needed to do and now she could go home. And she could think.

The only negative thing about that was her own mother. There'd be no escaping her scrutiny and Lucy wondered how long it would be before that astute woman noticed something was very wrong indeed with her daughter.

Dominic walked away from his parked car and stood at the far edge of the field, watching the three of them enjoy the fireworks about twenty metres away. It had only been three days since he'd seen them, but it felt so much longer. Chloe and Abby were dancing with excitement and Lucy stood beside them, her hair blown about her face and colour in her cheeks. Her eyes were focused on the huge splashes of colour bursting in the sky, her hand gently resting on Chloe's baby-fine hair.

It twisted something inside him. He hadn't seen her look like that for weeks and, God forgive him, he hadn't even realised it before. She looked happy. Her eyes were sparkling and she was laughing.

He'd meant to walk over and join them but he couldn't bring himself to do it. He didn't want to see her face change to the wary, shuttered look she habitually wore around him. He'd meant to persuade her to stay with him, to negotiate a new start—it was why he'd come. But how could he? She was like a released bird.

This was where she belonged, where she was happiest.

He watched as Chloe said something to her and Lucy knelt down on the muddy grass and rubbed her knitted gloved hands between her own. He didn't doubt he could make her stay by playing on her love for the girls, but he couldn't do that to her. Not now.

'Daddy! Daddy!' Abby caught sight of him and ran across the field towards him.

He hunkered down and opened up his arms to receive her.

'Did you see the fireworks? Did you?' His daughter bombarded him with questions.

Dominic stood up and waited for Lucy to join them. Her nose was slightly red from the cold and her dark hair feathered around her face. As he'd predicted, all the naturalness left her and she appeared stiff and guarded. Silently, he squared his shoulders and met her with a quiet, 'Hello.'

'I didn't know you were coming here.'

He reached down to stroke Chloe's face. 'I didn't know myself until this morning.'

'Is something wrong?'

Chloe tugged at his sleeve. 'We're going to have hot dogs and baked potatoes.'

'There's a stall over on the other side of the field, behind the bonfire,' Lucy explained, pushing her hands down into her coat pockets.

Dominic's hand curved around Chloe's but his eyes never left Lucy's. 'It's a bit early for bonfire night.'

'I know. St Cath's always does a display in half-term. One of the governors is an expert.' She gave a half-smile, swift and without much humour. 'He's the local vicar, actually.'

'Dominic! Lucy didn't say you were coming up.'

He turned to look at Lucy's mother. 'It was a spur-of-the-moment thing.'

'I see.' She glanced across at him and back to Lucy, her round eyes taking in her daughter's pale face. 'Why don't I take the girls across to get the hot dogs?' she suggested.

'We could all go—'

Dominic longed to reach out and touch Lucy's face, to remove the cold, anxious look in her eyes that had appeared the minute she'd known he was there. But she didn't want that. 'I'm not hungry.'

'Well, you take Lucy home,' the older woman said decisively. 'I'll take the girls back to mine after the hot dogs. You can pick them up later. It'll give you some time to yourselves.' With one child on each hand, she led them inexorably across the field.

Dominic watched Lucy as she watched the girls disappear into the crowd. 'Do you want something to eat?' he asked, forcing her to turn to look at him.

'Not particularly.' She pushed her hair firmly out of her eyes and he could see her make a decision to appear relaxed. 'I didn't realise you'd have finished all your work by now.'

'I haven't.'

'I could have—' Her dark eyes swung up to his. 'You haven't? Then why—?'

He shrugged. 'I didn't know where you'd gone, Lucy,' he said quietly.

'But I left a message with Fionnula!'

'Ah, yes. Fionnula.'

Two lines appeared between Lucy's eyebrows. 'Didn't she tell you?'

'Only that you'd left.'

'Oh.' She didn't understand. He could see it in her eyes.

'We had a row.'

Lucy nodded, but he could tell she still didn't understand what he was trying to tell her. She didn't know Fionnula had flounced back to

London, claiming she'd no idea where the 'fashion disaster' he'd married had gone to. She didn't know he'd driven back to London expecting to find her at home and that Fionnula had lied. Or that he'd spent three hours on the telephone trying to track down Jessie in the hope she'd know where she was. Or that he'd driven up here because he had to see her. And, looking at her now, he couldn't tell her.

'I'm so sorry. I should have spoken to you myself but Fionnula said she'd be seeing you at dinner and you didn't like to be disturbed when you were working.'

Dominic found his hands could still curl uncontrollably into fists. It was as well for Fionnula that she wasn't there. Nothing of that showed on his face. He took a deep breath and said calmly, 'When I couldn't reach anyone at the house I got worried.'

Lucy bit down on her lip. 'I'm sorry. I forgot my mobile too. How did you find us?'

'Jessie.' Dominic looked at her hungrily. It was as though he hadn't really looked at her for weeks—not since their wedding night. 'And then your neighbour said you'd be here for the fireworks. When I saw all the cars I wondered whether I'd be able to find you.'

'It's very popular...' He heard the shaky breath she drew before she asked, 'Why are you here? You could have phoned me at home.'

Home. Her use of that single word crystallised in his mind what he already knew. This was her home. Shropshire. The place where she'd been happy with Michael. The place where she wanted to be.

'I wanted to see you, to talk to you... I didn't mean to make you unhappy,' he stated simply at last.

'Is that why you're here? I'm fine.' Lucy's mind was swimming in treacle. In her mind there was only one cohesive thought—*she was pregnant with his child.* She had to tell him about the baby. Did he already know? Had Jessie told him something?

'That's not true, is it? You're unhappy—and so am I.'

She pulled her coat closely around her body, uncertain what to say.

He sighed, as though he was searching for words. His handsome face was drawn and he had the look of a man about to shoot his best friend. 'I know how depressed you've been since...since the wedding. I meant to persuade you to stay but...'

But? Lucy felt the blood drain from her face. 'But?' she managed through lips that didn't want to part.

'I think it's time we faced up to where we are.' His voice was resigned. 'I'm sure we can work something out.'

She wanted to scream at him, to shout, *But I'm carrying your baby,* but her mouth wouldn't work. All the while she'd been making her plans she'd forgotten that Dominic would be making his own. 'Do you want to end our marriage? Is that it?'

He sighed heavily and pulled a hand through his windswept hair. 'I think we can find a way to care for the girls without stifling our own lives. It's time we stopped this.'

So this was it. The moment when she discovered whether she could actually let him go. Did she love him enough? Her eyes travelled over his face. The same kind eyes she'd first been attracted to were watching for her reaction. What was he feeling? Pity? Did he know she loved him? Was this why he wanted to end it now—before they'd even reached the court case?

If she told him about the new baby he'd stay. The temptation was strong, but she had to resist it. It would be better to give him a chance of happiness. She'd manage. If he believed they could work out a system to share Chloe and Abby he'd be able to do it for this new little life. To tell him now would make him feel guilty.

'Why now—before the court case? Is...is it Fionnula?'

'Of course not.' He sounded exasperated.

'I'm s-sorry. I just thought... I knew she was interested, that was all,' she finished lamely, fighting back an almost overwhelming urge to cry.

Behind her the bonfire burst into life. The crowd moved closer to where they were standing.

'We'd better move.'

Lucy looked round. 'Yes.'

Tacitly they turned to walk towards the gate. 'She was—is interested.' He looked embarrassed. 'But I'm not. I know Vanessa hoped...'

'Jasper told me you weren't interested.'

'Did he?' He shook his head, unbelieving of his own stupidity. 'I'd no idea until she tried to make me believe you'd left me. I'm sorry. I should have known.'

'It doesn't matter now.' Lucy opened the latch and pulled the gate wide.

'She wanted me to believe you couldn't cope with life in London and had left.'

'I hadn't.'

'No.'

'I wouldn't do that without speaking to you first.' *But she hadn't told him about the baby.* Her conscience was whispering that it wasn't fair. She ought to give him the choice. But if she was right—and he stayed married to her because of the baby—she couldn't live with that. 'But she's right, I suppose. I've not coped well with life in London.'

'It doesn't suit you.'

'You need someone who can do all your entertaining. Someone who enjoys it. I do understand. We can still do what's best for the girls.' She didn't know how the words were coming out of her mouth so calmly.

'And they've had a chance to get to know each of us as well as each other.'

Lucy led the way down the country lane, now incongruously filled with parked cars because of the firework display. 'So it's been worth doing.'

'Definitely worth doing.'

She drew a steadying breath. This was excruciatingly painful. She felt as she had when the doctors had first told her about Michael's condition, and again when she'd heard Chloe wasn't her biological child. It was that same sense of pain that went too deep for any outward show to do justice to the agony. 'So what now? Do you want a divorce?'

Dominic raised the collar on his leather jacket to keep out the cold. 'Eventually, perhaps. I'm obviously in no hurry…'

'I don't know anything about divorce. How long does it take?'

'We don't have to rush it. Obviously, we'll need to sort out the money.'

'I've got money. I've got my house—'

He cut across her. 'We could try and find a couple of properties close together in the country. Maybe something with a building plot. Share a garden, perhaps? Would that be awkward?'

What he was suggesting sounded like the latest in twenty-first century torture techniques. To see Dominic and know she could never have him would be impossible. 'It might be if you marry again.'

'Or you do.'

Lucy looked at him. She couldn't ever imagine that, but there was no point in saying it now. She had a baby to carry and give birth to. *His* baby.

They turned the corner and walked up the tiled path to her front door. 'So…what do we do now?'

'I go back to Northumberland and work my way down the country, as planned. It's slightly more complicated now Fionnula's gone back to London, but I'll manage. When I get back you can start looking for somewhere you'd like to live.'

And the new baby? She turned the key in the lock and walked inside.

'Obviously, if you meet someone else then we'll have to speed things up.'

Lucy turned to look at him. Standing inside her narrow hallway he completely overwhelmed the space. She took off her coat and laid it gently across the back of an old balloon-backed chair. 'I'm sorry there's nowhere to hang anything. The hooks fell off months ago, and I never got round to putting them back, and then—' She broke off on a sob, turning her face away.

'Lucy? Wh—?'

It was over. Everything she'd hoped for was completely ended. They were being so dignified, *so reasonable*, but she didn't feel like that. She was scared and frightened and angry and— sad. He didn't love her. *Couldn't.*

'Don't! Lucy, don't cry,' Dominic's arms came round her and held her against his chest. 'It will be all right. I'll think of something. I should never have forced you into this marriage. I'm so sorry.'

It wasn't his fault. She wanted to say something that would comfort him. 'From the beginning you told me you couldn't love me. You—'

'I was an idiot.' She raised a tear-stained face to look at him, surprised by the vehemence in his voice. 'I *am* an idiot. I'd give my life to make things right for you.'

'Would you?' she whispered, mesmerised by the intensity in the blue eyes that held hers steady. She knew she had all the pieces of the jigsaw but she couldn't quite piece them together.

His arms tightened about her and she suddenly found she was being kissed. Her head fell back on the support of his arm and she stopped worrying about the whys and wherefores. She only knew he was kissing her as though he

meant it. Dimly, her head was instructing cau-
tion, but she couldn't quite stop the seeping
happiness that had already started to dissolve
the pain.

Dominic pulled away to look down at her
face. 'Don't go, Lucy.'

'I—'

He wouldn't let her speak. 'I mean, don't go
now. Don't go ever. I need you and I love you.
I should have told you before but I didn't know
it.'

Tears began to trickle down her face, welling
up before falling in heavy droplets.

'I know that wasn't part of the arrangement.
I know I told you right from the beginning that
I didn't expect love to be part of our marriage.'
His thumb wiped the damp trail from her face.
'I wasn't lying to you. I didn't expect it. I don't
know how or even when it happened, but I do
love you.'

He straightened up and gently held her to
face him. 'I know you've been unhappy, and I
haven't done anything to make things easier for
you. I should have seen what Fionnula was doing. I'm sorry for that. If you want your freedom, then…then I'll understand that.'

Her whole soul was filling with sunlight. 'And if I don't?'

Dominic's hands closed convulsively on the tops of her arms, his handsome face softening with an incredulity that made her feel all powerful.

Lucy reached out her hand and lightly traced the firm curve of his jaw. 'I love you,' she said, slowly and deliberately. 'I've been unhappy because I couldn't believe you would ever feel the same about me, and I—'

His hands jerked her towards him, pressing her body up against his as his mouth descended. 'You mean it?'

Lucy smiled against his lips and he felt it. He gave a shout of pure triumph as he twisted his hands through her hair and turned her face up to look at him. 'I should have told you as soon as I realised how I felt about you. I think I knew even before our wedding how much I loved you. It made me feel so guilty.'

'Because of Eloise,' she said sadly.

His arms tightened around her. 'In part, but also because I'd promised you a paper marriage. I felt ashamed of the way I was feeling about you when I knew you hadn't been widowed very long.'

Lucy laid her head on his chest and listened to the comforting beat of his heart until she felt brave enough to ask, 'Was that why you told me I'd been a mistake?' Even though she'd taken care to make her question sound nonchalant she could hear her pain rip through the air.

'Not you. Never you. You were incredible. Did you honestly think…?' He shook his head, unbelieving. 'I said what I thought you wanted to hear.'

'Why did you think I wanted that?'

'Because you cried.'

Lucy frowned. 'When?'

'After we'd made love. I saw you cry and I knew you were thinking of Michael. I knew I'd taken advantage of you when you were vulnerable—'

'No.' She shook her head.

He looked bemused. 'No?'

'I cried because of you. Because I knew I loved you, and what we'd just shared had been so amazing. I knew I could never be Eloise, but I thought…'

'I don't want you to be Eloise.' He moved his thumb to rest gently on her lips. 'I did love her, and I will always love the time we had together and the memory of her. Just as you will always love Michael.' He smiled down at her. 'It took me some time to work through everything, but I've finally got it. If we hadn't known them and loved them we'd have been completely different people.' He kissed her lightly. 'Now we're these people. The people they made us. And the person I am now is head over heels in love with the person you are now.'

Lucy could feel she was trembling on the edge of tears. 'So what do we do now?'

'We make up for all the time we've wasted. We go back to London and put the house on the market and look around for something that suits us both.'

'For the people we are now.'

'Absolutely. A completely new start.' He smiled, the glinting smile she hadn't seen in weeks. 'So, Mrs Grayling, are you going to keep me standing about in the hall or are you going to take me somewhere I can show you just how much I love you?'

Lucy hesitated. There was still one thing she had to tell him. 'On one condition.'

'Name it.'

'That you promise to be there when I wake.'

Dominic pressed a gentle kiss on her forehead. 'You've got it.'

Her voice wavered slightly. 'You see, I might need you in the morning to bring me up a cup of tea and a dry biscuit.' She searched his face for a glimmer of understanding.

He started to speak, and then changed his mind.

'I'm going to have our baby. I know I should have told you—'

'Our baby?'

Lucy nodded nervously. 'I was going to tell you, but then you said you wanted to leave... Are you angry?'

His hand slid down to rest on her stomach. 'How long have you known?'

'Not long. I came here to think. I didn't want you to stay with me because of the baby. If you didn't want to be married to me I wanted to let you go with a clear conscience.' A tear slid down her face and she bit her lip.

Dominic groaned and cradled her tightly against him. 'You're an amazing woman, Lucy. I love you so much.' He laughed and pulled away. 'I can't believe it! Our baby?'

Tremulously she smiled, daring to believe his happiness. 'Yours and mine.'

'You know, I like the sound of that.' He curved his hand around hers and led her to-

wards the stairs. 'Have you got any other sur-
prises you'd like to get out of the way?'

'Not that I can think of.'

'In that case,' he said, pausing to kiss her in
a way that made her stomach somersault, 'take
me to bed. From what I remember of babies,
we'd better not waste a moment!'

EPILOGUE

Lucy looked at the seventeenth-century beams of the home she and Dominic had chosen together with complete satisfaction. They still gave her a thrill, almost making her forget the months of dust and builders that had nearly driven them both mad.

Her emerald-green evening dress swished against the polished floorboards as she bent to pick up the primary coloured baby-walker that had migrated into the hallway. Life had really changed.

'You look beautiful,' Dominic said, coming up behind her and wrapping his arms around her waist. 'As ever.'

'Do you think I'll do?'

'I think—' he spun her around to face him, his eyes glinting mischievously '—you scrub up very well, as Jessie once said. In fact, so well—'

She put up a hand to ward him off, letting it rest lightly on his dinner jacket. 'No time.

284

We've got an award dinner to go to, remember?'

He moved his head to kiss her neck. 'Now I know why women wear their hair up. It means I can just—'

'Stop misbehaving,' she scolded as shivers of pleasure rushed down her spine. 'That kind of behaviour can get a girl into trouble. Just make sure you've got your speech. I don't want you to embarrass me.'

Dominic straightened and checked his pocket. 'You know if I don't win you won't get to hear my speech?'

'Is it good?'

'It's important,' he corrected, his eyes suddenly serious.

Lucy frowned. 'Why?'

'Because,' he paused to take her face between his hands, 'if I don't win you won't get to hear me thank my wife for giving me back my life…and I want her to be absolutely certain what she means to me. Without her I'd be nothing. I'd like to thank her for our girls, Abby and Chloe, and for our boys, Benjamin and Edward.' He gently kissed her. 'And any more God sees fit to send us.'

'You're welcome,' she managed.

'And I'd like to give her this.' Dominic reached down in his jacket pocket and brought out a narrow black velvet box.

She took it gently, her eyes questioning. 'What's—?'

'Open it.'

Lucy flicked open the delicate clasp and looked back up with shimmering eyes.

'I'm told it has freedom combined with intense security.' His voice deepened. 'It's in the way the gold sweeps round to hold the diamond.'

'It's Jasper's necklace.'

'Ours now. I saw the sketch again the other day and I asked him to make it for you.' His mouth twisted in a wry smile as he lightly touched the dark shadow of her cleavage with his forefinger. 'And I thought it would look perfect nestled just here.' Then he kissed her. 'You're my diamond, Lucy.'

'I love you,' she whispered.

Dominic smiled the smile that always made her feel slightly giddy. 'I love you back.'

MILLS & BOON® PUBLISH EIGHT LARGE PRINT TITLES A MONTH. THESE ARE THE EIGHT TITLES FOR MARCH 2005

———————— ❧ ————————

THE MISTRESS WIFE
Lynne Graham

THE OUTBACK BRIDAL RESCUE
Emma Darcy

THE GREEK'S ULTIMATE REVENGE
Julia James

THE FRENCHMAN'S MISTRESS
Kathryn Ross

THE AUSTRALIAN TYCOON'S PROPOSAL
Margaret Way

CHRISTMAS EVE MARRIAGE
Jessica Hart

THE DATING RESOLUTION
Hannah Bernard

THE GAME SHOW BRIDE
Jackie Braun

MILLS & BOON®

Live the emotion

0205 R